BRIDE PRICE

26

26

Also by J.N. Catanach

White is the Color of Death

BRIDE PRICE

A mystery by
J.N. Catanach

A Foul Play Press Book

The Countryman Press
Woodstock, Vermont

First Edition

Copyright ©1989 by J.N. Catanach

Library of Congress Cataloging-in-Publication Data

Catanach, J. N.
   Brideprice: a mystery/by J.N. Catanach.—1st ed.
      p. cm.
   "A Foul Play Press book."
   ISBN 0-88150-125-5
   I. Title.
PS3553.A8193B7 1989
813'.54—dc19

                                 88-30157
                                   CIP

Book design by Leslie Fry
Typesetting by the F.W. Roberts Company

Printed in the United States

A Foul Play Press Book

The Countryman Press
Woodstock, Vermont
05091

Marion: thanks

A ripping sound agitated my left eardrum. I woke up. It was the air hostess (in those days they were still called that) leaning across to raise the shade. "Landing in a few minutes, Miss. You haven't filled out your forms, have you?"

Then, almost at once, a voice over the p.a. system, "This is the captain. We are just crossing the Equator."

I turned, and literally caught my breath. Framed perfectly in my window was Mount Kenya, silhouetted a deep grey against the lightening sky, its base wrapped in cloud; an auspicious welcome indeed. We approached the mountain until the white of its topmost glacier stood out, and the black of its jagged peak and the green of its forested slopes. Looking down, I began to see the occasional road, fields neatly delineated, clusters of roofs—round and square, thatched and tin—ridges deeply gouged by streams, all passing beneath us; like us, making the slow descent to Nairobi and the plains which stretch three hundred miles to the Indian Ocean. To the right loomed the dark, forested mass of the Aberdares, and beyond, lost in cloud, the Great Rift Valley, the walls of which formed the boundaries of a world a version of myself had once inhabited.

I applied myself to the forms.

Name: *Stephanie Duncan.*

Nationality: *British.*

Country of residence: *Canada.*

Date and place of birth: *3 September 1955. Kenya.*

Purpose of visit:

Here I paused, gnawing on the ballpoint. Suppose I told the truth? I wrote, *Tourist,* and closed my passport. Then I opened it again, near the back, and took out a scrap of paper. I stared hard at the scrap, something I'd been doing a lot lately, holding it close, then at arm's length, as if trying to divine some secret. It was a photo of a car snapped from behind, neatly snipped from a newspaper—some time ago, judging by its condition; a car which appeared to have plunged down a bank into vegetation. No date, no caption or credit, just a number, partially obscured, painted on the near door: 45? 46? 48? I couldn't even tell the make.

I was just a few days into my twenty-second year. But young as I was, and uninteresting as I felt, I was about as old that year as I'm sure I'll ever be, and life was far from dull, as far from dull as I think I ever want it to get.

ॐ

The sign said, WELCOME TO NAIROBI—CITY IN THE SUN. Only, of course, there was no sun at that season of the year. Nairobi was wrapped in its customary blanket of grey. "*Karibu nyumbani*," the official had smiled as he stamped my passport. "Welcome home." But it didn't feel like a homecoming. Not yet. Not on the airport bus. No doubt, at some point, it would. After all, I had spent half my life here, hadn't I?

I don't care for bougainvillea. I especially dislike it on roundabouts. The bougainvillea on the round-abouts on the Embakasi Road is trained to grow over barbed wire, reined in, clipped close, colorful in a picture-postcard way. And in ten years they seem to have added more roundabouts and therefore more bougainvillea and more color. The traffic slowed. Up ahead I could see flashing lights. An accident. On a roundabout. As we snailed by, the dismal scene un-folded: car versus motorcycle. A tartan rug covered something on the grass, only a hand protruding.

"Oh, brother," I thought, mindful of the cut-out photo. Abruptly I looked away. Two rows back across the aisle a man's eyes were on me, an interrupted stare. For an instant we held each other's gaze, shar-ing something painful, so it seemed. I turned away and didn't look back.

CHAPTER TWO

I'm at the Y. The YWCA. It's a little bit up the hill from downtown. Walking distance. And cheap, considering meals are included. Which means I eat all three here or starve. And I have a job. It took three weeks, and I've not been paid yet. But now I'm free to launch Phase 2 of the operation, which is why I'm here.

Up to a couple of days ago I made no attempt to contact anyone who'd known me before. For a while, anyway, I wanted to be incognito. Why? I guess the feeling of standing on the edge of a lake of virgin snow appealed to the Canadian in me: if there were tracks, I wanted them to be mine, or to know who or what made them. There was to be method in my quest.

When I was ten my parents drove away and disappeared out of my life. Yes, drove away. They waved goodbye, and never came back. And I was packed off almost at once to live with a distant relative in Sudbury, Ontario. I had never forgiven those who plunged me into that misery and blankness. No explanations. No answers. My guardian refused to talk about it. On the face of it I might have been a stray who'd inconveniently turned up on her back porch. One day in school in my second year in Canada I took a felt-tip pen and wrote on the back of my hand 'I am alone.' My teacher was deeply shocked. My guardian grimly ordered me to wash it off.

Tonight I made my debut, so to speak. Came out. Spread my wings. I chose Gillian. Gillian was my best friend at prep school. Letters had ricocheted between the continents for a couple of years, petering out as we had less and less to share, dwindling into Christmas and birthday cards and silence. Her letters yawned with omission, not telling me what I most wanted to know and was afraid to ask outright: about Mum and Dad. When I called her parents' number, someone—her father, I think—told me how to reach her. I was glad it wasn't her mother, who would have wormed out of me things I wanted to keep quiet, like my name.

So Gillian was caught off guard. She had a new name: married for a year, she said, to someone I didn't know. Yes, everything was great. She asked me to dinner "to show off my house and my hubby." He would pick me up Friday on his way home from the office.

Friday was today. It's almost over. This is the quiet time at the Y, when one can think, when the shouting and door-slamming, the blasting tape-recorders and the loudspeaker with its jarring squawk are all hushed, by order. My cubicle—room would be exaggerating—overlooks the parking lot of a new block of flats. A bombax tree stands stiffly limbed against the fresh whitewash. Bolt upright on its stone surround sits a helmeted soldier-of-the-night, greatcoat buttoned to the ears: the watchman. But for the occasional glow in the bowl of his pipe he might be carved in wood. From somewhere beyond comes the yowl of the Siamese cat that night after night upbraids an increasingly exasperated audience, leaving one to feel that its days are surely numbered.

Opening night. How did it go? What had I learned about my parents? At this point any tossed-out scrap seemed a princely portion to one as starved as I.

Richard—the "hubby"—strode through the front door of the Y at the appointed hour. From my gloomy corner I was able to observe him with impunity for a few seconds. He had the panicked air of one out of his natural element, as indeed his club tie, natty blazer and slicked back hair proclaimed him to be. The front hall had a tobacco-juice brownness about it—walls, furniture, pictures, floor. The fake exposed beams hinted at mock-Tudor; the pervasive stench was of floor-wax and boiled cabbage; the cluster of noisy females at the pay phone were in varying states of preparation for a big night out. I came forward, glad for his sake to be wearing my only skirt.

"Stephanie? Good-oh." He seized my hand and shepherded me out as a fireman might lead someone to safety from a burning building. "Phew!" We were in the car, a gleaming sporty model. "What masochistic impulse drove you *there*, pray?"

"It's called poverty."

"Oh." He looked at me briefly and turned the key in the ignition. "We'll have to see about that, won't we." He wasn't that much older than I, yet exuded the fatherly air of one for whom anything is within reach. "Gillian *is* looking forward to this."

But Gillian, I think, was disappointed. She really had been looking forward to showing off and showing *me* off. (Hadn't she always, all those years ago, and hadn't I made the perfect foil?) I could tell the way her mind worked: here she had all these treats for me and I proved unworthy, didn't measure up. I was fresh from ten years in North America, hub of the sort of lifestyle she yearned for, and what did she see before her? A frump. (I don't want to be down on myself, but I really don't care too much how I look. My wardrobe was simple to the point of being stark, befitting an orphan without 'expectations.' The idea of adornment seemed unexciting. It was vaguely understood that a few pieces of jewelry from my mother had been 'put away' for me, but the time to claim them seemed never to come.)

Gillian certainly hoped for something more glamorous. She herself ran to the plump and pretty, with a beautiful fair English skin and blond hair, elegantly coiffed and only a tiny bit touched up for color. She wore an expensive, somewhat frilly maternity dress.

We lounged on the verandah of their comfortably sprawling house on the edge of town. From our feet the grass sloped gently some hundred yards to a watercourse marked by a thick ribbon of trees. Cloudy

mornings were being followed by clear late after-
noons, and now the setting sun glinted on the tin
roofs of dwellings that dotted the plain beyond the
trees. Gillian noticed it too. "Bloody Masai," she
said. "Spoils the view. Why can't they stick to
thatch?"

Richard shielded his eyes and peered south across
the plain. "You should have been here yesterday.
Kilimanjaro deigned to show herself. No such luck
today." Was I imagining, or did his wife's comment
rankle? I'd gathered in the car that he was out from
England on a temporary posting with his company.
A catch indeed.

"Darling, she's not a *tourist*," Gillian rebuked.
"She's seen Kili billions of times, and a darn sight
closer." Gillian looked to be about eight months
pregnant; her face, under its layer of make-up, still
conveying the sulkiness I remembered. "Isn't it
about time for a drink?" As if on cue a white-robed
figure in a red tasselled fez emerged from the house.
"What'll it be, Steph?"

"G & T?"

"I'll follow suit."

Richard jumped up, muttering something about
'giving the old boy a hand.'

"He's gone to ration out my gin." Gillian patted
her stomach. "Little does he know what we get up to
between nine and five." I remembered, too, the con-
niving grin.

All the while in the back of my mind I was thinking, how will it come up? It has to sound natural,

incidental. Little dialogues skipped through my mind. Gillian: 'How *awful* for you about your parents . . . ' Me: 'Quite a shock at the time, naturally . . . ' Gillian: 'But to have them both go like that, in one fell swoop . . . ' Me: 'One adjusts at that age; you know, I don't even know where they're buried.' Gillian: 'Dad and Mum could tell you, I'm sure . . . '

Gillian was talking. "I said, they're coming for dinner."

"Sorry, who?"

"Dad and Mum. And that tiresome Munson person from Ravine. You may remember. She's staying with them. Down for the Show."

The servant had re-emerged. I took the proffered drink. "*Jambo, Memsab.*" He was still bending, holding the empty tray, peering expectantly at me.

"*Jambo,*" I saluted, awkwardly.

Gillian burst out laughing. "You don't recognize him, do you! It's Hongo."

"Hongo!" I scrambled to my feet, spilling some of the drink. Gillian's parents' old cook! The times we'd had together. We shook hands warmly.

"He's asking if you've got yourself a good man, like Bwana Richard," Gillian translated. My Swahili was rusty indeed.

I shook my head. Hongo spoke again.

"Hongo, you old pagan. *Kwenda, kwenda.*" In mock anger Gillian shooed him away.

"What did he say?"

"I'm not sure I should tell you."

"Oh, go on."

"He said Bwana Richard should take you for wife number two." Richard went red to the tips of his ears and drained half his whiskey. "Mum gave me Hongo for a wedding present. I rather suspect," Gillian confided, "he's her spy in our camp. She knew about this"–patting her tummy–"long before it was official."

Hongo. One avenue I hadn't considered. I wondered if my Swahili was up to it.

Dinner was like a tug-of-war: me against the rest. In the end I gave up and treated the whole thing as a game, a sort of verbal grandmother's footsteps; seeing how near I could sneak up on the subject of my parents before they–and they did act like accomplices–looked round and immobilized me. "And how are things at Ravine?" I turned to Mrs. Munson. She and her husband had farmed not many miles from us and as such were a detail in the tapestry of my growing up.

"Very grand these days, thank you," her voice boomed like a tidal wave across the polished table, setting the crystal tingling. Its extraordinary timbre was attributed by my father to a penchant for whiskey and cigars. "Blacktop all the way. You must come and stay with me. I insist, my dear. There are compensations for having a cabinet minister or two as neighbors. And the *fences*. You've never seen such fences. Ten-foot chainlink for miles and miles. You'd think we had Borstals everywhere."

"Beyond Nakuru it's all Royal Family, I believe," Gillian's mother put in eagerly. "The Old Man on

10

BRIDEPRICE

one side of the road and daughter Margaret on the
other. The joke is there's a few hundred yards un-
fenced where some old Kipsigis tribesman won't
sell. Isn't that right, Eric?"

Gillian's father squirmed. He was something se-
nior in one of the ministries, a civil servant and
a bit of a stuffed shirt, I'd always thought. "The
trappings of power, my dear, in this case well de-
served." To speak of the Royal Family here meant
the Kenyatta family. "Whatever we thought about
Jomo once upon a time, we wouldn't be sitting here
now if it wasn't for him."

"But some of them go a bit far. Pinching whole
forests. Your own minister, Eric, you said so yourself . . . "

"That's quite enough, Louise." She wilted under
his glower. He held up his glass, "To Mzee Jomo
Kenyatta, President of Kenya. Long may he live."

We sipped in silence. Hongo noiselessly cleared
plates.

Over coffee and brandy, taken around a fire in the
living room, I made a fool of myself. I think it was
sheer exasperation. To no one in particular, apropos
of nothing, I blurted, "You know, I don't even know
where they're *buried*." No one in particular answered. It was the general signal to leave.

I said goodbye to Gillian's parents and to Mrs.
Munson, who insisted again that I stay with her upcountry. Then, mumbling something about thanking Hongo for the meal, I slipped into the kitchen
before leaving.

11

"Hongo," I said, and—dredging up sufficient Swahili—I asked him for news of the two servants who had come with us from the farm when we moved to Nairobi.

"*Sijui, Memsab.*" I don't know.

"*Hapana jua kabisa?*" Don't know *at all?*

Perhaps sensing my need, he slowly shook his head, a commiserative gesture. I waited. The open window over the sink at which we were standing gave onto part of the driveway. The guests were walking to their car. A single sentence, in a whispered boom, trundled across the gravel: "Do you mean to say she doesn't *know?*"

Hongo put down the cup he was drying. "I think, *Memsab,*" he said in English, "you must ask at the place of *Bwana* Storrito."

"Storrington?"

"*Ndio, Memsab.*"

"Does the name Storrington ring a bell?" I asked Gillian on the way out.

"Storrington? Wait a sec. No. Why?"

"Don't worry. I'll check the phone book."

And that was that. My debut.

The soldier-of-the-night has risen and is marching round the tree with deliberate stride; a latecomer has driven in. I think, Japanese. Statistic: there are ten times the number of foreigners in Kenya today as thirteen years ago at *Uhuru*, Independence. More Brits, even. They are all making money, or dispensing it.

Before me on the table is the square of newsprint I

keep in the back of my passport. I pick it up, turn it over. The words on the reverse indicate it is from a local East African paper. Yet it arrived in the mail in Sudbury on the morning of my twenty-first birthday, the address typed, the postmark Toronto. I imagine the picture is of the car in which my parents were killed.

CHAPTER THREE

I remember waking up in my room at the Y on my first morning back in Africa and the realization, the slow dawning, that for the first time in my life I was beholden to nobody. To come home at a reasonable hour, to be at the other end of a phone, to be somewhere other than where I was, were obligations discarded. I could be sick, in danger, at risk, fat, wear outrageous make-up; in short, do as I pleased. Whether Stephanie Duncan lived or died was nobody's concern but her own.

Or so I thought.

On weekdays at the Y anyone not in the dining room by seven sharp might as well resign themselves to a breakfast of fried bread and baked beans washed down with tea; the fruit would have been eaten. On Saturdays when the population dwindled a little more leeway existed. Accordingly, on the morning after Gillian's dinner, although it was nearly eight, I was able to spear a couple of slivers of paw-paw and a chunk of pineapple to slink off with to my usual corner.

"Who's the boyfriend?" Yvonne, an Australian

about my own age who seemed to have adopted me, plunked herself down.

"Boyfriend?" I was puzzled.

"Last evening; in the Porsche." Yvonne's frank brown eyes sparkled appreciatively in their galaxy of freckles. From the little I'd come to know of her she had a single preoccupation: men—or rather, the perfect man, preferably, of course, rich. She'd taken a couple of years off, she said, to work her way round the world hunting for 'Mr. Right.' In fact I was surprised to see her here at all on a Saturday. Her affairs of the heart—which lasted a week on average—were usually at their red-hot peak on Saturdays, blew apart volcanically on Sundays, and Mondays found her moping, bruised and cut-up, over her fried bread. By Monday night she'd have bounced back and be planning the ascent of the next male Everest. I hated to disillusion her about myself.

"You mean *Richard*. He's married."

"Naughty, naughty," she wagged a delighted finger at me across the greasy yellow cloth.

"To my best friend from prep school."

Yvonne hooted gleefully. "Oh, you bitch, you."

"Only he's not my type, I've decided. I guess I'm not into Porsches."

"Trade you a favor for his work number."

"I'll think about it."

We had both arranged to get mail poste restante, and, after breakfast, wandered down to the main

15

post office, fifteen minutes away across a grassy park, a six-lane highway and a couple of city blocks. In three weeks nothing had come for me, nor did I see why anything should, so I was surprised to see the clerk returning with something: a Canadian air letter in an all too familiar hand.

Yvonne was already deep into a long dispatch from Australia, and it was with a sort of curious dread that I tore into mine. Heads down, we crossed a sliproad and stood reading on a narrow traffic island as cars whizzed along Kenyatta Avenue inches from our toes. " . . . nor need you have troubled yourself to thank me for that which was by no means my doing," my guardian had scribbled in the stilted way she was wont to address me, as if I were an inanimate object like a dead canary or a Grecian urn, "unless I am taking literally what was intended as irony. The supposed subtleties of your nature have ever eluded me . . . " I had merely thanked her in a brief note for paying my air fare to Kenya. She seemed to be saying she hadn't.

I looked up, aware of a sudden outburst of hooting across the avenue, or perhaps it had been going on for some time. A car had stopped dead in the middle of the far lane causing a jam. Yvonne looked up long enough to aim a chestful of laughter at the lowering sky—someone in Australia must have cracked a joke. She resumed her reading.

I tried to reconstruct events surrounding the purchase of my plane ticket. The day after my twenty-first birthday, I had—without telling my guardian (I had never shown her the mysterious clipping of the car)—gone to the travel agent in Sudbury to ask about Nairobi. The regular round-trip fare came to roughly four times my savings, so we worked out a cut-rate convoluted scheme via Buffalo and New York City to London, where I would have to scrounge some sort of employment to finance the rest of the journey. I'd be lucky to be in Kenya in six months. In the afternoon I quit my job at the florist. That evening I told my guardian I was leaving the next day. I don't think she believed me. "You can't," she said flatly, "you have nobody to go to."

I'd got as far as New York when I was paged over the airport intercom. A reservations agent told me that my ticket had been paid right through to Nairobi. The only conceivable explanation was that my guardian had awakened to the seriousness of my intent and—eager to place as much distance between us as quickly as possible—had gone to the travel agent with a check. I thanked my stars and thought no more about it. Now, poised on a traffic island in Kenyatta Avenue, her letter fluttering in my hand, it seemed I must assimilate a new and unexplained facet of existence: had I exchanged a guardian for a guardian angel?

"Look at that man in the car over there—he can't keep his eyes off me." Yvonne self-consciously smoothed down her light cotton skirt.

I followed her gaze. The car that had almost caused the pile-up had pulled over to the far curb and a man was leaning from the window. Only he wasn't ogling Yvonne; he was staring at me. "Yvonne, I forgot," I said, "I have to check a name in the phone book here; the one at the Y's in tatters." I dodged back into the post office.

Storrington, Storrington ... There was no Storrington in the Kenya phone book. I cursed myself for not pressing Hongo on the subject of Storrington. Perhaps I'd heard him wrong. Stonington? Staringon? Sherrington? The prospect of a second visit to Gillian's loomed distastefully. Tap, tap, tap. I stiffened. A knocking on the wall of the phone booth. Yvonne? She had joined a long line for stamps. Tap, tap, tap. Someone in a hurry to use the phone, no doubt. I closed the book and stepped out of the booth into the presence of a diminutive East Indian in a cloth cap. The air of meekness and long-suffering that suffused him elicited from me an apologetic smile. But instead of heading into the booth, he responded with a polite half-bow. "Miss Duncan?"

I was so surprised, I said, "Yes."

Gravely he proffered a little white card. I glanced at it. The name meant nothing. "Perhaps you would do my master the honors to go with me." He gestured towards the street.

A little desperately I looked around the room for Yvonne, wondering in some back chamber of the mind whether I'd have to scream. She was some way off, still in line. "Really, I don't think so, thanks all the same," I mumbled, backing away. The man looked hurt. "Perhaps another time," I foolishly added, dodging through a gap in a line which closed comfortingly behind me. The man made no attempt to follow. He stood for some moments, gazing abstractedly after me, and when I sneaked a second look, was gone.

"Yvonne, quick, let's get away from here." I yanked her out of line and propelled her towards the furthest exit; for all I knew, the man would be back with reinforcements. "The weirdest thing just happened . . ." We crossed Kenyatta Avenue and dived into Koinange Street, heading for the municipal market, Yvonne all agog at the drama and kicking herself that she'd missed it.

"White slavery," she embellished, when I asked what she thought. "No doubt about it."

"But he knew my name," I challenged. Yvonne seemed to think the whole thing was a lark.

"Oh, sure; but this is Con City, didn't you know? There's ways he could have found out."

"Such as?"

"Such as when you asked for your letter; he could have eavesdropped. Or when you were reading it on the street, he could have peeped. I'm telling you, they're pros. I'm going to have to clue you in some time, kid."

She had a point, of sorts. "Then why did he give me this?" I dug in my jeans pocket for the little white card and waved it in her face. "A name, an address, a phone number."

"Could be a phony; he could have picked it up anywhere." She took the card. "Hmmm. I wonder if he's cute. May I keep this?" I snatched it back.

We meandered through the market looking at fruit and vegetables and fish and all manner of tourist trinkets. But the incident in the post office had cast a pall over me. We had climbed the stairs to the balcony that runs round the inside of the building and were examining some Masai spears when—testing the weight of one—I happened to glance down its shaft into the body of the market. In all the color and hubbub a man stood quietly, his hands in his jacket pockets, not moving, staring up right into the point of my spear. My hand shook.

"That's the man in the snazzy car," Yvonne exclaimed, pointing. "Not bad, eh? Bit old, but then a touch of grey is nice in a man, stability, confidence . . . " She prattled on. I watched him turn away and make his way slowly between the stalls. He didn't look back.

"Watch out with that," Yvonne shouted. I was still holding the spear.

CHAPTER FOUR

A gold-colored sportscar, engine purring idly, crouched in the driveway of the Y. The few girls in the lobby who seemed to have nowhere in particular to go this Sunday morning eyed it hopefully. One or two took compacts from their purses and dabbed languidly at their faces.

Yvonne had come to my room in great excitement and dragged me forth to view the pulsating vehicle. Something told her, she confided, that here was the man who would rescue her from the desert of her sexless weekend. Whoever he was, assuming he *was* a man, he had not been seen to enter the Y, though his golden chariot quivered emptily only yards from the door. "So where's he hiding?" Yvonne sniffed around.

We walked as far as the road to investigate. Nothing doing. One or two cars passed. The usual quota of pedestrians padded silently along the verges. Another grey Nairobi day. I felt dispirited, which, part of my mind told me, was ridiculous: I'd hardly begun to do what I'd come to do. How could I even think of giving up. What was I afraid of, all of a sudden? I've always felt that more than one voice spoke inside my head, and if I could get a discussion going, in the

21

end things composed themselves. While I tried thus to pinpoint what exactly the matter was, Yvonne ran a finger along the body of the car.

"Sleek," she commented, caressing the driver's seat through the open window. It appeared to be upholstered in some kind of animal skin.

"I thought you were anti-fur." She had a poster over her bed of a stylish woman in a fur coat with the caption, 'Wouldn't *you* kill for this?'

"Quite, and somebody's a bad boy." She opened the door. "What say we go for a spin?"

"Hop in."

The voice behind me sounded reassuringly relaxed and very British. I swung round. It was the man from the market. He stood with his hands up in an attitude of surrender, a faint smile creasing the corners of his eyes. I glanced at Yvonne who had turned a distinctly red face in his direction.

"A precaution," the man lowered his arms. "A spear in the ribs ... one never knows in Africa ... there are less painful ways of leaving this world, wouldn't you agree?"

I returned his smile in spite of myself, though ruefully I imagine. "I'm sorry. I was only holding it, and you appeared at the end."

"Ah yes, of course."

I grew bolder. "I must say, you seem to make a habit of it. Appearing, I mean." At close range, I had to admit there was something endearing about the man; it had to do with his eyes; penetrating, under dark lashes, but fundamentally kind. His quiet air contrasted with the car which, I assumed, was his.

"The bad penny? But this time I have a perfectly rational explanation. I just hopped over the fence there to have a look at something." He indicated the block of flats beyond the bombax tree. "I have a small interest in that property. But perhaps we should introduce ourselves. You are Miss Stephanie Duncan, daughter of Major and Mrs. Duncan, formerly of Nairobi, are you not? I am Kassim Salim, your humble servant." He bowed slightly, but made no attempt to shake hands.

Yvonne coughed. "And I'm Miss Yvonne Dent." She had moved up to stand beside me and from this vantage point had been studiously batting her eyes at the man. He now acknowledged her existence with a courteous nod.

"But how on earth did you . . . ?"

"I had the honor to be acquainted with your parents. We shared a number of interests . . . "

"But yesterday . . . " I stammered idiotically.

"Yesterday I experienced an extraordinary shock. Forgive me if I acted foolishly. When I noticed you—quite by chance, by the way—outside the post office, I thought I had seen a ghost. You have the looks of your mother, you see." He shook his head. "It is quite remarkable."

"No," I mumbled, "I mean I didn't know. I was quite small when she died. I was sent away. Actually I've no idea what she looked like. I haven't even got a photo."

"Not even a photo?" He was clearly nonplused.

"Well, we'll have to see about that. I wonder—I know this will seem a trifle sudden—but would you, and of course your friend," he smiled at Yvonne, "care to join me at my house for lunch?"

"No really, we couldn't possibly . . . "

"Oh, come on," Yvonne coaxed. "Sure we can."

I don't know why I hesitated. Perhaps because it all seemed such utterly smooth sailing, just the sort of break that minutes before I'd despaired of. My nature is to be suspicious when things go well, concentrating on the inevitable hitch rather than savoring the moment of ease. I stalled. "How did you know I was staying here at the Y, or was that chance too?"

He had a moustache which drooped slightly at the corners of his mouth; he stroked these droopy ends with thumb and forefinger. "You will think me quite shameless, Miss Duncan. I had you followed." I looked about, half expecting to see the little man from the post office hovering nearby. "No, I'm all alone today."

Yvonne decided it was time she took matters into her own hands. "It'll be a tight squeeze," she declared brightly, addressing the car. "This wasn't what you were driving yesterday."

"No. I have a different one for every day of the week."

Yvonne's eyes widened. She whistled. Whether she believed him or was trying to play Lois Lane to his Superman I wasn't sure. "I'll be OK in the middle." I was sure she would be. It was a two-seater.

Our new-found friend hastened with mannered courtesy to open the passenger door. Yvonne edged up against the stick-shift. I shrugged, allowing fate its head, and climbed in after her. Kassim Salim, smiling politely, carefully closed the door. Yvonne nudged me and winked.

"I'm so hungry I could eat a horse," she announced once we were under way. She had a way of running her sentiments up a mast like flags.

"Roast beef and Yorkshire pudding—the Sunday lunch of the British. Yes, twenty years ago I was up at Oxford. But I'm afraid you will be disappointed." Neither Yvonne nor I had been to England, let alone Oxford. We drove north, away from the city center, by winding, tree-lined roads. The feeling possessed me of having travelled them before, though I couldn't pick out specific landmarks.

"Didn't we live out this way, in the old days?"

"You don't remember?" He sounded surprised.

"Kind of, but it's all a bit hazy."

"Then I will show you, if your friend's stomach can stand a slight delay? A conducted tour of your childhood." The notion seemed to amuse him.

"We weren't here long," I said defensively. "In Nairobi, I mean. A year or two at the most."

"At that age a year is a lifetime."

"Funny—I remember more about the farm, even though I was younger."

"Perhaps you were happier there." He changed down, adroitly avoiding contact with Yvonne's calf which she was doing her best to entangle in the

25

gearshift. We left the highway and bumped a short distance along a dusty side road. The houses here stood back behind insubstantial gates and long strips of jaundiced lawn. A line of Australian blue gums—like giant sprouting telephone poles—seemed to have sucked the green out of the landscape. I recalled the aromatic smell, the dusty roots and curly papery bark sensed as I trotted to school in the mornings.

The car stopped. "Is this it?" I asked, "really?" The house at the end of the drive was not the somber Hansel and Gretel monstrosity I remembered, but a black and white gabled, faintly ridiculous, quite harmless edifice which might have sheltered a dentist in Sudbury.

"Shall we pay our respects?"

I shook my head. The gate was open, but there was no sign of a car. The doors of the double garage were closed.

"Possibly the signor and signora are at church. We could go in for a closer look."

"Thanks, but I'd rather not." Even to my own ears I sounded prim. Then it occurred to me to ask, "Why, do you know them?"

"No, but I can read." He pointed. The usual *'Umbwa Kali'* warning was wired to the gate, but up against the straggly hedge bordering it was another weathered inscription: *'Dominioni de Doriano Santoretti.'* Santoretti? Storrington? A possibility.

As we bumped away, Yvonne remarked that it seemed like a nice house to grow up in. I said nothing, and sensed that our host, for whatever reason, understood my silence.

His own compound was a few minutes away on the other side of the Ngong Road—the main artery leading north out of town towards the Rift Valley. At the end of a short driveway was a tall slatted gate set in a brick wall. Our host tooted the horn and we waited. In a little while, to considerable scraping, one half of the gate began to jerk toward us revealing a scrawny individual in a brown robe and cap. When he had pushed it far enough he went back for the other side. Kassim Salim watched impassively. When both sides were open to his satisfaction, the gatekeeper stationed himself appropriately and, with the drilled dignity of an old soldier, snapped a salute. He could well have been brother to our old Sudanese watchman whose cane—to the horror and fascination of my young eyes—concealed a sharp blade.

We found ourselves in a shady courtyard whose floor of packed dirt was spattered lavender blue with jacaranda petals. The lord of this manor jumped out and strode around to open our door before I could even find the handle. I'd have flopped out into the dust had not his strong hand steadied me. The look on Yvonne's face made me scowl. It said, 'Hey baby, not bad, you're learning.'

A door was opened by an unseen hand. We were ushered into the house. I'm not much good at descriptions, but the impression I had was of walls caparisoned with rich tapestry and ornaments of silver and ivory and brass cluttering every available surface. Our host led the way along a passage and into a spacious room, bare by contrast, blessed with a gorgeous Persian carpet. My eyes were drawn across its expanse to a plate glass window taking up an entire wall and giving onto a garden in which I saw orange trees. Lured by the spectacle of this earthly paradise, I descended two or three steps to the carpet and looked out into what I now perceived was a glassed-in courtyard with brightly colored birds hopping among the foliage.

Our host had remained by the door; turning to compliment him on the splendor of it all, I caught an expression on his face which alarmed me: a sort of trancelike absorption in which I appeared to be the focus. I changed my mind and kept quiet. Yvonne's face was already pressed against the pane. If he noticed my unease, Salim seemed not at all disturbed by it. "Do you play?" He indicated a concert grand off to his right. It was white with gold trim.

"Sorry."

He turned and bent over a wooden cabinet in the wall. I caught the silvery glint of stereo equipment as he pushed some knobs. All at once, from goodness knows how many concealed speakers, emphatic, deep piano notes marched forth. "Please." Smilingly he indicated the piano stool. I obliged, an obedient actor now in this weird mise-en-scène. Chopin's *Marche funèbre*. I closed my eyes and gripped the stool.

28

Under the spell of the music, I saw myself upstairs in my room after supper. My thoughts were full of homework. 'A Trip I Took This Hols,' 'A Day in a Game Park,' along those lines. The notes from downstairs that forced themselves upon my consciousness, at first so deliberately plodding, took on a poignance, as if the clouds had cleared above the climber's head to reveal a patch of lucid blue. Drum rolls became trills. Then the climber seemed to surrender effort, defy weight, take flight, the soul leaving the body. I longed to be that climber. Then back to the plod, only with hope, quieter, and that funny last note of all, like a question mark.

CHAPTER FIVE

Mercifully, we did not have to listen to all four movements of the B flat minor Sonata. My mother, anyway, had never tackled more than the march, at least not in my hearing. She had taken up the piano rather late in life, after we moved to Nairobi from the farm, slogging away at it without seeming to tap into any kind of natural talent so that I've often wondered why she persevered. But as with all she undertook, she struggled gamely, refusing to admit defeat. I say 'late in life,' but that's a ten-year-old's perspective; she was barely thirty. I always associated the piano with those last two years of our lives together and it makes me sad. We had no piano at the farm.

"How did you get to know my parents?" We were seated—Kassim, Yvonne and myself—at a glowing mahogany table to which a young attendant had conveyed a succession of curry dishes, each tastier than the last. To Yvonne's vociferously expressed delight, few concessions to Western practices—such as cutlery or toned-down spices—had been made. Greasy-chinned, she chased morsels around her plate with bits of pourri bread while our host, seemingly delighted with our responses to his hospitality, eyed us benevolently and ate little himself. When the exclamations and explanations that attend this sort of feast had died down, I decided it was question time. He knew a surprising lot about me. I wanted some answers from him.

"Shared interests, as I mentioned." Kassim moved his glass, which contained passion-fruit juice (no alcohol was in evidence), an inch to the right as if it were a chess piece on a dangerous mission, then leaned back and observed it critically. "Rally driving mainly. Your mother was a great driver. We would run into each other at various do's around the place; and at the Club, of course, after they graciously consented to admit a less than lilywhite member of the human race." He shot a smiling glance at me, but it was Yvonne who responded.

"Christ, what swine." Her liberal hackles rose to the defense. "Neanderthals."

Kassim accepted this declaration with silent amusement. He was shades whiter than freckled, sun-browned Yvonne. Judging by an enormous signed photo of the Aga Khan that I'd seen in the other room, he was a member of Kenya's small but prosperous and influential Ismaili community.

"Would that have been the Nairobi Rally Club?"

He nodded. Memories crowded back: of an eight-and-a-half year old I'd done my best to forget being dumped in a playground full of insultingly juvenile contraptions like swings and slides while my parents chatted endlessly at the bar of the adjacent

31

clubhouse. I was awkward, indignant, defiant; an only child used to adult company, a wild thing from upcountry struggling to come to terms not only with city life but with parents who now seemed intent on escaping from her. Even now, confronted by this apparent rival for their affections, I felt an irrational resentment inject itself into my emotions. "Do you still drive, in rallies I mean?"

"I must confess it's been a while. But I have my collection to keep me company in my declining years. If you like, I'll give you the tour."

Yvonne, again, came disastrously to the rescue: "You don't look a day over thirty. Well, thirty-five."

"Very kind of you, but I wouldn't want to be young again. Forty is quite acceptable." Far from declining, Kassim, at that time, seemed a man at the peak of his powers. He turned to me, "And while we're on the subject of age, what brings you back to the land of your birth, may I ask, Miss Duncan?"

From my capacious, all-purpose pouch bag I produced the newspaper clipping of the car. He studied it impassively for a good minute. "I see."

"Do you?" The eagerness of my response seemed to startle him. He handed it back.

"Miss Duncan, how much are you aware of the circumstances surrounding your parents'–uhm– tragedy?"

"To be honest, I'm a total blank. I was told nothing at the time. And please, you don't have to tip-toe. It's been ten years."

"Ten years," he mused. "Yes, I suppose it has been."

"I was whisked off to Canada to live with a relative I'd never met—a cousin of my mother's—who carried on as though my parents had not existed; which was fine, up to a point. One can adjust to almost anything, it appears, at least superficially."

"Up to what point, may I ask?" He observed me with peculiar interest, head slightly cocked, like a bird observes a worm it is about to devour.

"The urge to clear things up, I suppose. I'd like to know, and get on with the rest of my life."

"A sort of spring cleaning, then?"

"I suppose."

"And that?" He indicated the clipping which Yvonne was now studying.

"It turned up among my guardian's papers. All I have to go on, really." Why I lied I don't know except that his eyes, boring into me, willed me to seek protection. Yvonne gave me a funny little look—I'd told her the true version—but she didn't blurt it out, thank goodness.

"So on the strength of that little scrap of paper ... " The idea seemed to appeal to him. "And how far have you got in your quest?"

"I'm here, aren't I?" I looked around the dining room, one wall of which, as in the piano room, gave onto the inner courtyard. "And if you'll shed light on that photo, I'll be that much further." I suspected he knew what it depicted; I also guessed that if there'd been a way out at that moment, he would have taken it. But we were both gazing at him, two pairs of earnest eyes.

"It's their car all right."

"How can you tell?"

"The number, for starters. 48. Besides," he smiled, "how many tanks like that were chuffing around Kenya, let alone competing in the Safari? You recall the East African Safari Rally?"

"They were number 48 in it?"

"Why yes. But surely you knew . . . "

"Knew what? I told you I know practically nothing."

"About the accident?"

"They drove away and never came back; that's all I ever *really* knew. Of course, one assumes things . . . "

"Miss Duncan, the photo you have here," he picked it up and waved it, "is of your parents' car after the crash. No doubt at all. Their Humber Super Snipe."

Humber Super Snipe. How rich the words still sounded; like Christmas Pudding. The glowing dials, the grain of the polished wood, the smell of leather, the armrests that went up and down, the tiny curtains, the little green-shaded reading light, the slipperiness of the back seat where I could curl up, my little house on wheels. And yet, something spoiled the memory. I was standing with our cook at the bottom of the drive, waiting. It must have been early evening, the time between daylight and dark, and I peered down the road in the direction of the roundabout. Others waited too, in little groups, chatting and laughing. I, alone, was deadly serious. Every few minutes two pale orbs glimmered towards me. Then came the roar of the passing car. Two people per car. Always two. Intent, grey figures, paying no attention to us. At last, *"Nakuja, nakuja! Bwana na Memsab! Angalia,* Steppy, *Bwana na Memsab!"* And our cook was waving as if his life depended on it. I screwed up my eyes and raised a tentative hand. My father's unmistakable, Toot-toot, toot-toot-toot, tooot tooot tooot; my mother blowing me a kiss; and they, too, were gone. I wanted to stare after the vanishing tail lights, but the cook had other ideas. He hurried me back up the drive as thunder growled in the distance. *"Mvua takuja."* It is coming on to rain.

I picked up the clipping. It looked nothing like the car I remembered. "Humber Super Snipe. Yes, it's starting to come back."

Kassim rose from the table. "Come," he invited, "I promised to show you my collection. A little surprise for you."

"Him and his little surprises," Yvonne giggled.

We followed him through a series of rooms mostly stuffed with ornaments, one of which boasted a richly canopied bed like something Good Queen Bess might have slept in. Yvonne surreptitiously tested the mattress. For all the splendor a sense of abandonment, of disregard, hung about, as if waiting had lasted too long. Was there a wife and family, I wondered, stashed away in some other wing, perhaps? No trace so far of domesticity.

At last Kassim flung open a door and stepped

aside for us to enter. I could tell from the smell, almost before I saw them, what was there. Cars. Various shapes and sizes. Like in a show room. We passed a number of shiny vintage models. Luckily Yvonne made all the right noises. Cars as art objects bore me. Kassim stopped and turned. "Humber Super Snipe." He ran his hand affectionately along the black bulge of the hood. I could only stare.

"It's not, I mean, the one . . . "

He understood. "I'm not a morbid man, Miss Duncan. Even had it been salvageable. I'm sentimental perhaps, but not morbid."

Yvonne had lingered by a sexy little racing number near the door. Now she joined us. "Why would anyone think you morbid?" she cooed to Kassim.

"It's all right, Yvonne." I came to his rescue. "I was just being assured that this is not the car my parents were killed in."

Kassim stared at me. "Your *parents*, Miss Duncan?"

God, I thought, what now? It was the way he emphasized *parents*. "Well, isn't that what happened?" It came out as a sort of challenge. The sight of the Humber had rattled me more than I cared to admit.

"Your mother, yes. Your father—but surely you know this?—your father survived."

"It's a lie," I screamed. I couldn't seem to stop screaming.

CHAPTER SIX

It had taken me ten years to adjust to the fact that I was an orphan. My anger, directed at two dead people, seemed almost to have fizzled out, like an arrow, I suppose, which pierces nothing but air. Then suddenly I am told, 'By the way, only one of those people is dead.'

Later that day Yvonne, in her languorous way, gave her version of what happened there in the garage. "You freaked out, Steph; and that's putting it mildly."

"Spare no detail." I knew she wouldn't, because she was mad at me.

"We were standing by the car, three reasonable people having a conversation, and the next thing I know you're *inside* the bloody thing, in the back seat, throwing a tantrum—like a five-year-old. You just screamed and screamed."

We were on an after-supper stroll to escape the Sunday evening drear of the Y. Yvonne said she wanted to work the mashed potatoes out of her system. I had not been able to eat at all, but needed the air. Of all evenings at the Y, Sunday was the dismallest as inmates crept back to nurse their weekend

J.N. CATANACH

disappointments or gloat over undeserved triumphs. Our chosen road led uphill past the rather smarter YM compound (complete with pool), and Yvonne very likely hoped that some handsome hunk might be hanging around sent by the gods to pluck her weekend from the abyss I had dragged it into. For it was my behavior, she intimated, that had scotched her chances with Kassim.

"Specifics," I demanded.

"You were pummelling the front seat like a prize fighter; and butting it with your head."

I recalled the heady smell of leather. Perhaps that's what set me off. It's a known fact that smell can trigger a memory. "And?"

"Poor old Kassim. You had him really worried; he didn't know what to do."

"He tried to climb in after me."

"You're imagining things. He was trying to comfort you and you bit him."

"Bit him? You're the one with the imagination."

"He had the mark on his hand. He showed me."

"From the door."

"Which you slammed."

"Anyway, I don't want to talk about him. I don't want anything more to do with him."

"I don't get it, Steph. You came here to find out about your folks. Here's a guy who can really help, and what do you do? Slam a car door on his hand."

"OK, OK. I was upset."

"Upset? You were hysterical."

It was no use trying to explain to Yvonne some-

38

thing I didn't understand myself. Poor Kassim. He probably *was* pretty startled. I had a dim recollection of his promising to do everything in his power to help; telling me, in fact, that my troubles were over and that he, Kassim Salim, would personally find out for me everything I wanted to know. But the one thing I needed to know at that point was what happened to my father: if he wasn't dead, where was he? Kassim professed ignorance. And the thing I couldn't possibly explain to Yvonne was this: I *wanted* him dead. I was locked into my belief that he was dead. I couldn't adjust. I couldn't deal with him alive. Not yet, at any rate.

No young hunk, or hunk of any age, lounged outside the YM and yearned for Yvonne. Unable to face a return to the YW just yet, she decided we should drown our sorrows in a film.

"But, Yvonne, I don't have the money; I'm not paid till next week."

Yvonne loaned me ten shillings. We walked downtown and wept quietly through the second half of something called, I think, *Pete 'n Tillie*. While waiting tearfully for the first half to begin we avoided eye-contact, until the ridiculousness of our respective plights hit us both at the same time and we found ourselves laughing.

"It's not working, is it?" said Yvonne. "Film therapy. It's disgusting the way everyone's in love."

The coffee shop at the Hilton was still open and a further substantial loan secured me a banana split with all the trimmings. Yvonne ordered a jumbo float in three flavors. "You've got to pamper yourself once in a while," she declared. "Good for the self-image. After all, that's the really vital thing; let that go and you're through." We stared out of the window at the lamplit empty street. "Penny for your thoughts."

"I was thinking of all the buildings that have gone up since my folks were around. This place, for one. I think it used to be the bus depot."

"What were they like?"

"My folks? Wow." I'd never been asked that before. How on earth do you describe your parents? "Pretty ordinary, I guess."

Yvonne was not going to be shunted off with that. "Come on, you're not even trying."

"Well, it's tough; narrow it down a bit."

"Did they have a good sex life?"

"Jeez, Yvonne, you and your one-track mind. I was ten years old. I didn't know what sex was."

"And you lived on a farm?"

"That was different."

"A late developer, huh? When I was ten I knew it all. I had older brothers."

"I didn't have any brothers. I just had Gillian to speculate with."

"The first time I came across my parents going at it I thought they were having a fight. I'd been across the street playing at the neighbor's and walked in on them rolling around on the hearthrug in the living room grunting and growling. Naturally I tried to break it up but they both yelled at me to go away; strange, I thought. After that, whenever the hearth-rug was missing I got suspicious and listened at their bedroom door. It was a tiger my grandad shot."

"Kinky." I was thinking about the fights *I'd* over-heard. At the farm we'd been spread out, a number of mud huts, really, strung together, which made for privacy. But in Nairobi we were all on top of each other. Nothing of love in those frightful night en-counters: my father often drunk, my mother defen-sive. As likely as not something would get broken and I'd catch Samweli, our houseboy, mournfully sweeping up the pieces as I left for school in the early morning.

"Was she easy to get along with, your mum?"

My mind's eye swept back across the years like a searchlight in a desert trying to pick out some fea-ture, anything. A thrill of panic seized me. A pilot friend had once tried to explain what it was like, in a small plane, to 'lose the horizon.' That's a bit how I felt.

Yvonne was staring at me. "Dearie me, as bad as that."

It was the little jolt I needed. All at once I saw the two of us together, myself, aged about five, looking down at my mother's face in terror and reproach: I was sitting on a horse, and she was laughing at me. "No, no; we had some good times together."

"And your Dad?"

"Oh, he was great," I said quickly. "Just great."

Yvonne ran a finger round the inside of her dish and sucked it noisily. "Mine is the pits, the absolute pits."

We set out disconsolately for home. Not much was moving in that part of town save cars. "We should get us a car," Yvonne said after a bit as if she'd solved some pressing problem.

"Why?" Cars—it seemed to me—cause more problems than they solve.

"Because I'm sick and tired of depending on *men*." The last word flashed out with excoriating sharpness.

I was glad for the cardigan I'd brought and pulled it round me as we waited to cross the avenue. "Do you think the park's safe?" There was plenty of artificial light about, but the path skirted some shadowy clumps of bushes.

"Let's find out." The alternative was a long walk around by the road. But the question of safety evaporated, chased from my mind by Yvonne's next observation: "So you could say you're lucky, in a way."

"How come?"

"Well, I mean the one you liked best lived."

CHAPTER SEVEN

"Yes, Miss Hickle."

The door to the inner office closed, not with a slam, but hard enough to set the glass panel jingling. Let us say, *firmly*. Firm, at any rate, is a Hickle word. She had, in fact, just used it: "One must be *firm* with these people, Stephanie." 'These people' tended to be anyone that Miss Hickle disapproved of, but particularly—in her capacity as Headmistress of the Nairobi Girls Academy (formerly the Princess of Wales High School)—parents or prospective parents. The parents in question this Monday morning happened to be Ugandan, the father a powerful official in the ruling Idi Amin regime, who had written requesting that their daughter not return to Kampala for the Christmas holidays but be put up at the school, 'due to the unsettlement of the times.'

"If we gave our girls board and lodging every time somebody said 'coup' we'd end up running a hotel," she huffed, after dictating to me a polite refusal. "I don't care what they call themselves, Field Marshalls, Emperors, it simply won't wash." Nor did it. Cabinet ministers with school-age daughters had

43

been known to tremble before Miss Hickle's piercing, blue-eyed gaze.

As one of the two watch-dog-cum-secretaries in the outer office—the only one that morning who hadn't had the foresight to call in sick—I was into my third attempt at typing an error-free letter to Uganda when I became aware of another presence in the room. A man stood at the open door. He stood so impassively that at first he seemed not quite all there, as if waiting for the rest of him to catch up. "I'm sorry." I flashed my office smile, strictly a movement of the lips, "Can I help you?"

"No, no. Please pay no attention until you are ready." He was a small, stoutish individual in a brown suit that disclosed a lot of cuff and hardly any shoe. His neck, what there was of it, was circled by a thin noose of a tie into which, at intervals, a rumpled shirt collar was tucked. His hair, parted deeply in the middle, lent a certain old-world flair to an otherwise nondescript appearance. I tried to place him: parent? Not aggressive enough. Teacher? He'd hardly have survived the pitiless students in that get-up. Job-seeker: cook perhaps, or groundsman? Too self-assured. Someone from the Ministry of Education? Too early in the morning. A contractor? The man about the gym windows Miss Hickle had mentioned? Aha, that must be it.

Damn. Another mistake. I dabbed on the eraser fluid, blew on it and typed in the identical letter, cursed silently and dabbed it out again with the fluid. The man, meanwhile, was softly circling the room although I swear his feet weren't actually moving. My desk was centrally placed, a sort of bunker against any frontal assault on Miss Hickle's sanctum. Soon he would be out of my line of vision. I ripped the copy from the machine. It was all his fault. "If it's about the gym windows, I'll take you over now.

A gurgle of amusement escaped his lips. "I am disturbing you. But no matter, you are wasting your time."

He now had my full attention. "I beg your pardon?" Now and then I catch myself doing a Miss Hickle.

The visitor retrieved from the floor a discarded attempt at the Uganda letter. "It is no use writing to this man here." He placed it on my desk.

"Oh?" I said coldly.

"He is not at this place."

"Why, are you acquainted?"

"You did not hear VOK news this morning? Amin has given this man to the crocodiles."

I knew what *that* meant. "Oh my God, the poor girl." I stood up. "I better tell Miss Hickle."

He looked at his watch which involved considerable adjustment of the cuff. "It is better to go first to the gym."

"Oh, all right," I conceded. Just as well to clear the decks for the impending crisis. As we crossed the green, myself striding ahead, he managed to hand me a grubby card. 'Wellington Waki Oloo,' it read, 'Private Eye for Hire.' "You do windows as well?" I asked, a little mystified.

"I try, if at all possible, to shed light." When I looked at him he was smiling sweetly.

We were both out of breath as I let him into the gym. "If you don't mind I'll leave you to it. Miss Hickle told me she wants the estimate in the post as soon as possible."

"Miss Stephanie." I was halfway out the door. "I have not come about the windows."

"You have *not* come about the windows?" I blinked at him stupidly. A sheepish look hovered on his face.

"I have come here because your Miss Hickle is not here so she cannot cause difficulties. It is a delicate matter," he explained, doubtless sensing my alarm and compounding it. "My client, who wishes to remain unknown, has put me at your disposal, to find out everything. So please inform to me now the place and time of our meetings so that I will not detain you."

A pretty speech. Once over the shock, I felt like applauding. So Kassim had been as good as his word. "And what do you intend to do, Mr.–" I looked at the card, "Oloo?"

"With respect, this is my business."

"Well,"–what did I have to lose?–"how about Fridays? I expect you know where I live? After work? That'll give you a day or two."

The break bell sounded. In seconds the campus was a tumult of girls in green and grey uniforms; given cameras and a director it would have made a great Shakespearian battle scene. Wellington Waki

Oloo melted into the fracas and I fought my way back to the office.

Miss Hickle was standing by my desk. From her long, ringless white fingers dangled nine sheets of paper—my three failed letters to Uganda and the six carbon copies. "Are you *intent* on bankrupting us, Stephanie? Do you *know* what we pay for paper in East Africa?"

I mumbled that I didn't. The only piece of paper that really concerned me at that moment was my paycheck, which seemed suddenly remote and unattainable. Then I surprised myself: "But, Miss Hickle, we can save on stamps." I passed on the news I had just heard about the crocodiles. Miss Hickle, who thrived in a crisis and deteriorated between-whiles, sprang into action. Silently I thanked the odd little man in the brown suit for the fact that I still had a job.

I did not, however, for one instant fool myself that Wellington Waki Oloo would be able to help me. I saw him strictly as a face-saving gesture on the part of Kassim Salim who had, in a moment of emotion, made a promise, and who doubtless looked upon himself as a man of his word. Unless—and it only struck me as I was going to bed that night—unless he could find the servants who had accompanied us to Nairobi from the farm, Mugwe the cook and Samweli the houseboy. Yes, I thought patronizingly, that would be right down the little fellow's alley. And since I wouldn't be seeing him till Friday—if he showed up at all—I'd make a start next day after work by testing my Storrington/Santoretti theory. After all, Mugwe and Samweli were among the last people to have seen my parents together. There was no knowing what tidbits of information they might have picked up and kept loyally to themselves.

I dozed off thinking not of my own father as I'd done the previous night (inconceivable that, if still alive, he'd not been in touch over the years) but of the daughter of the Ugandan who had been 'given to the crocodiles.' She had sat in Miss Hickle's office in a composed, almost grown-up, yet unreachable state. It was not clear to Miss Hickle that she had taken in what had happened, perhaps had not quite understood. But I knew, and pitied her from the bottom of my heart.

CHAPTER EIGHT

As usual I was the only European on the bus and as usual it was sardines all the way so that even the pickpockets were having a hard time. I got off downtown and found a second bus which was heading up the Ngong Road, also packed. Uncomfortable and even panicky as at times I was, I admit to a certain exhilaration during these rides: they seemed as close to Africa as it was possible for a white girl in Nairobi to get. We were all workers together, little people bathed in a common sweat. I had to push and shove with the next person. On this particular bus getting off was the tricky part. First I had to worm my way to the back. The driver passed my stop. I tugged at an unresponsive bell. He zoomed by the next stop. I yelled. People around me yelled. He drove blithely on. Pretty soon everyone in the bus was yelling for me. The bus stopped. I got off leaving considerable merriment in my wake. I suppose nobody normally gets off that soon.

Trudging back in the semi-darkness with the headlights coming at me and coming at me, I thought again of my parents, of the last time I had seen them: on that bit of road at that hour. But I thought about them a little differently—their good-bye wave did not seem as final. And I had a question for Kassim Salim which I would probably never put to him because I did not want to see Kassim again; the question that had blown us apart at Gillian's, the question of graves.

As I stumbled, dazzled, along the rutted sidewalk, I was aware of an orange orb of light suspended among the gum trees across the road. I'd taken it to be a petrol sign—Esso or Shell—and actually had to stop and examine it before concluding that it was, in fact, the moon—huge and low and close, a doleful backdrop to what had been our house. How Africa distorts; two days ago I'd seen the house in daylight through Canadian eyes; here it was now in a child's African eye, its mystery restored.

I had to run to make it across the road. The gate, as before, was open. I stepped boldly into the domain of Signor Santoretti on the premise that the *umbwa* (dog) might prove less *kali* (fierce) in the face of self-assurance, even if only skin-deep. Again, no car in evidence and the garage wide open, only this time lit from within. A light isolated the front door. And then—or was it just in my tired head?—music. 'How did you get on with your mum?,' Yvonne had asked. It was as though I was about to find out.

I was home from school later than usual; perhaps we had been on a field trip, I can't remember. Mum was alone in the house. It must have been about a year after we'd moved from the farm. Usually I for-aged around for my own supper, but this time she helped me and sat down to watch me eat. "If Daddy or I had to go somewhere for a long time, which of us would you want to be with?" She cupped her chin in her hands, her elbows resting on the dining-room table.

"You," I said, through a mouthful of cornflakes.

She didn't move her hands, but her cheeks glistened with tears. Later, on my way upstairs, I dragged a finger along the table top. It was still wet.

A woman opened the door, a chunky woman with a lined heavy face under dyed blonde hair, arms brimming with Pekinese. "Signora Santoretti?"

"*Sì?*" she frowned, as if expecting bad news.

I introduced myself, explaining that I'd lived in the house as a girl before going to Canada.

"You, Canada?"

I nodded brightly. It was not going to be easy. A Strauss waltz floated past us into the night. Word by word, alternately scolding and kissing the dog as it somewhat dutifully licked her face, she constructed a picture of why I was there.

"This your 'ouse. Please, please." She preceded me across the hall, an ample figure draped in a crocheted red shawl a corner of which trailed on the carpet; her slippers—wispy purple things—resembled a couple of dyed Pekinese. "My 'usband 'e come"—she mimed driving a car—" 'E English OK."

"If I could just talk to the servants . . . " I attempted. "Cook? Houseboy?"

"Cook, what for cook?" she exploded. " 'Ouseboy, what for 'ouseboy?" She pointed vigorously at herself, giving the Pekinese its chance to escape. "I cook, I 'ouseboy. You like eat?" she added more calmly, pressing her fingers to her lips.

I nodded. Too late for the Y. Might as well get something for my pains. Besides, a rather enticing smell was coming from the kitchen.

"*A momenti.*" She padded away trailed by the dog which gave me one last worried look, sensing a rival.

I waited. The room was strangely bare of meaning. I couldn't decide if it had been our dining room or the room my mother used as a work room. It was crammed with fluffy animals, at least a hundred. At last the sound of a car coming up the drive; the slam of a door; voices from the kitchen. A man entered the room, small, wiry, his head bald and brown as a hazel nut, a hand extended for me to shake. He waved me back to my chair and collapsed in one beside me.

"So you have come back to your roots. All Americans nowadays, they look for nothing but roots." I corrected him. "American, Canadian, same thing. We Italians, however, we are born, we make love, we die. For us, is enough."

Over supper, which lived up to its enticing smell, I learned that he was a freelance photographer and had spent the day at the Agricultural Show—the big event at this time of year—taking pictures at the Italian Pavilion. No, he had no idea till now who the previous owner of the house had been. He had bought it from a bank, unfurnished, a couple of months after he arrived in Kenya; July or August, ten years ago. Yes, two Africans had been living in the servants' quarters out back keeping an eye on the place. He had employed them until his wife joined him but she had never been one for servants in the house. (She nodded vigorously.) Now they just had a garden boy. He'd found the cook a job with an acquaintance in the Italian community who had just lost his wife; he lived out beyond the airport. He wrote out the address. The other was older and—he seemed to recall—had gone home to his location. He couldn't be sure.

Gallantly, he insisted on delivering me back to the Y.

On Wednesday I asked Miss Hickle what it meant when a bank sells you a house.

"I would hope it means that they own it."

"Yes, but how come?"

"What a question. Perhaps it was security for a loan which defaulted, or part of a bankruptcy proceeding, or the bank is simply acting for the owner; all sorts of reasons. Do I take it you are proposing to buy a house?"

I reminded her that I had not yet been paid.

Friday was a red-letter day. In the morning I was paid for two weeks' work. (I am rich.) In the evening I had a visit from Wellington Waki Oloo. At last a rent in the obscuring grey. I say 'Friday *was*' though it's not yet over: the Siamese cat is caterwauling somewhere out by the block of flats, the night watchman is watching the night motionless under the bombax tree. I feel that my mind hasn't yet absorbed the implications of what I have learned. Not much chance of sleep until it settles down . . .

CHAPTER NINE

In suggesting the Y as a meeting place I forgot the rule about visitors, which was simple enough: none permitted. And while the odd female slipped past the matron on guard, to my knowledge no male ever did. Wellington Waki Oloo was the sort of man to bring down the ire of the guardians of propriety upon his head: an air of meekness enfolded him; he was like a walking apology. His clothes were not 'styled,' his smile not artful, his car barely held together—though he'd had the sense to park it on the road out of sight. Here was a born victim. He was asked to leave.

No way were we going to sit in the lobby and be spied on after that. I looked questioningly at him, embarrassed. "It is better that we go to my office," he said evenly. We climbed into his old blue Volkswagen and had hardly gone two hundred yards up the hill before he turned off down an untarmacked sideroad and off that into the drive of an ugly squarish yellow building advertising itself in broken bits of ceramic tile as Club Jacaranda. I'd noticed it on one of my walks and it had always seemed closed. Wellington pushed open the door and in a couple of shakes we were seated on stools at a counter which showed signs—shelves without bottles—of having once been a bar. The room was strewn with rattan chairs and tall ashtrays. Nobody took the slightest bit of interest: there was no one around. At one point a youth entered, was waved at by Wellington in the vague and friendly fashion he sheltered behind, and withdrew.

With a silk handkerchief which had been hiding, unseen, in the breast pocket of his suit—the same brown one he had worn at our first meeting—Wellington wiped a portion of the bar and set down reverently upon it a new plastic attaché case. "Miss Stephanie Duncan," he intoned, patting it. From it he withdrew a number of Xeroxed sheets of paper, laying them out in some sort of order along the bar.

At that point the youth re-entered. "Telephone for sir," he announced importantly. Wellington slipped off his stool.

"The first thing for you is to read," he told me, "from this side." Picking up his case, he followed the youth out of the room. I was alone.

Perhaps it's best at this point to set down what I read in the order in which I read it. The pertinent passages, all copied from Kenya's principal daily, the *Standard*, had been marked in red.

Friday, April 12th. A banner headline, "THEY'RE OFF! MZEE WHISKS OFF THE LEADERS." Caption on accompanying picture: "The President of Kenya, H.E. Mzee Jomo Kenyatta, using his flywhisk, waves away the first car in the grueling four-day, 3,000 mile, East African Safari Rally." Circled in the text near the end of the story was the subhead, "OLDEST ENTRY." "Taking the cake for this year's oldest entry is number 48, the Humber Super Snipe of Dick and Helen Duncan, Safari perennials and the only couple competing as a team this year. The car has over 90,000 miles on it."

Saturday, April 13th. Headline, "DUEL TO THE DEATH. FLYING SIKH V. IMPLACABLE POLE." "By midnight last night only 21 of the 98 starters had limped back to Nairobi to ready up for the southern leg of what one old-timer has dubbed, 'the chocolate pudding Safari.' 'It was mud, mud, mud all the way and then some,' complained veteran Swedish rally-ace, Gunmar Gran, who ran out of road on the Tot-Tambach section and waited three hours for a tow. But all attention focussed on the dramatic duel for the lead that veteran local rallyists Joginder Singh and 'Nick' Nowicki were locked in almost from the start. The checkpoint at Meru measured only three minutes between these 'old men of the mud' as they flashed by around Mount Kenya racing to reach Nairobi. Because the unexpectedly early rains washed out some bridges, several last minute route changes were put into effect . . . " Circled was the subhead, "NOT ACCOUNTED FOR." "Among cars not accounted for at presstime were the Volvo of Mrs. Trehaine and Mrs. Cudlip which, according to other drivers, hit a man-made roadblock in Uganda, and the Humber Super Snipe of Dick and Helen Duncan which checked in at the Ena Bridge control south of

Meru with just minutes in hand but had not passed
through Embu. These two teams are most likely
spending a comfortable night in the bush."

Easter Sunday, April 14th. Headline: "TRAGEDY
STRIKES." "For only the second time since its in-
ception in 1953, the Safari has claimed a victim.
Locals in an area north of Embu, on the slopes of
Mount Kenya, this morning reported a car that had
plunged off the road into a ravine. When the police
arrived they found the body of Mrs. Helen Duncan
crushed behind the wheel. She had apparently been
dead for several hours. No sign was found of her
husband and co-driver, Dick Duncan. Police have
sealed off the area and speculate that Mr. Duncan
may have wandered into the bush looking for help.
A thorough search of the area is reportedly under
way.

"The couple were last seen alive when their Humber Super Snipe passed through Ena, where the control officer stamped their card. They reported no
particular problem, although, like everyone, were
running very late because of the appalling conditions, and had only minutes in hand before being
time-barred. But with the worst of the mud behind
them officials believed they had a sporting chance of
making it back to Nairobi in time to qualify for the
southern leg into Tanzania."

An accompanying photo was captioned, "Mr. and
Mrs. Duncan with their Humber Super Snipe at a
rally last year in Nakuru." It showed a man and a
woman posing front on with the car between them.

They were smiling a little diffidently, touching the Humber as if it was a shy child in need of reassurance. My parents! The man gave an impression of strength and impenetrability: square jaw, aggressive moustache, dark smoothed hair, dark slits of eyes and dimples that triumphed over the poor quality reproduction. My mother—hair dashingly held back with a scarf, sunglasses pushed up on her forehead—presented a 'let's get it over with' attitude to the photographer. I could imagine her tossing out one of her amused, slightly cutting remarks as soon as the shutter clicked.

Tuesday, April 16th. Headline: "THE UNSINKABLE SIX!" Buried in a story on the half-dozen cars that struggled back to a hero's welcome in Nairobi from the quagmires of Tanzania on Easter Monday was this circled paragraph: "This year's Safari was marred by the tragic death of Mrs. Helen Duncan when the car she was driving plunged off the road at about midnight on Friday a few miles north of Embu. Her husband and co-driver, Dick Duncan, has not yet been found but there is speculation that he is still alive. A search party, including a police tracker dog and scores of volunteers, is combing the area. It is thought that, in going for help, he may have stumbled in the dark into one of the deep ravines that scar the forested landscape."

Wednesday, April 24th. A small paragraph: "The remains of Mrs. Helen Duncan, who died tragically when the car she was driving went off the road during the East African Safari Rally, were laid to rest at St. Cuthbert's Anglican Church, Ravine. A few close friends were present. The whereabouts of her husband, Dick Duncan, who was believed to have been with her at the time of the accident, is still unknown. Anyone with information bearing on the accident is urged to come forward and give it to the nearest police station. Mr. and Mrs. Duncan's only child, a daughter, has left for Canada where she will stay with relatives for the time being."

'For the time being.' I shivered. I had a vision of my feet treading under me on grey, cracked concrete, then ascending some steps—I suppose, to the plane—and the pressure between my shoulder blades of a guiding hand. I was wearing red sandals.

Thursday, May 23rd. A question is raised in Parliament. "Mr. Jackton Mseme (M.P. for Meru South): Mr. Speaker, it is said in my district that Somali *shifta* have penetrated as far south as Embu, carrying off a European. The people are very much afraid and have asked for more police protection but so far nothing is being done.

"Mr. Ndungu Ndege (Assistant Minister for Home Affairs): Mr. Speaker, the police have no reason to believe that *shifta* have penetrated this far. Whatever *shifta* have not been chased back to their country of origin are being closely watched by the security forces in the North Eastern District. I would like respectfully to point out to the Honourable Member that it is the job of elected leaders to put out the flames of rumour, not to fan them.

"Mr. Jackton Mseme: Mr. Speaker, when I need

advice on how to do my job, I will remember to ask the Honourable Assistant Minister for Home Affairs. (Applause.) Meanwhile I am asking why this European has not been found by the police. If a European can disappear and not be found, people are very much worried that the police cannot protect them. (Shouts of 'Shame'.)

"Asst. Minister for Home Affairs: Let me assure the Honourable Member that the police are leaving no stone unturned.

"Mr. Jackton Mseme: Mr. Speaker, if the police were not so busy turning over stones, perhaps this case would be solved by now. (Applause.)"

Wellington had returned and was standing uncertainly at the far end of the bar. I wasn't sure what he expected of me, but I hadn't expected this of him. "Well," I said inadequately, "it's been an education all right." Relieved, he began collecting the papers. "But you've kind of left me in the lurch, haven't you?"

"You mean you have not been educated enough?"

"I mean, my father—What did happen to him?"

Wellington stuffed the papers into his attaché case. "All that I can find, it is here," he said sadly.

I foraged in my purse and handed him the clipping of the car. "What about this?"

He studied it. "Where did you find this?"

I told him of its mysterious advent. "It seems to be from a local paper. Where did you find yours?"

61

"I cannot divulge classified information." He smiled enigmatically. "May I keep this?"

I took back my precious clipping. It was my link, my only physical link with someone. It had become my talisman. "Surely there are ways of finding out? The police, for instance. They must have records."

He pitied me. "It is very difficult for you."

"Look, I'm not paying you. I don't have any right to ask you, but . . . " I stopped, close to tears.

"I am at your disposal," he said. "I shall try my best. Next week, same time, same place."

"Here?"

"If it is all right."

I refused his offer of a ride and walked home. Yvonne's door was locked. I knocked. No answer. So she's fixed up for the weekend, I thought. I resigned myself to my room, perplexed and lonely.

CHAPTER TEN

Saturday I worked a half day because I needed
the money and Miss Hickle 'desperately' needed me
(to lick envelopes, as it turned out). I returned to the
Y just in time to miss lunch, which didn't bother me
because the taste of the glue had made me nau-
seous. I had just lain down on my bed to recoup
when the p.a. system summoned me to the desk.

Gillian's Richard was pacing to and fro fingering
his watch. "Bit of luck to find you in. Was down at
the office catching up on a spot of work and it just
occurred that you might like a ride out to the Show.
I'm meeting Gillian and co. there and they'd be absolutely delighted . . . " He was a little red in the
face.

"If you hang on a sec, I'll run and put something
respectable on." Funny, only yesterday I'd have
turned him down flat. I found a clean blouse and
pair of jeans and joined him in the Porsche.

We hadn't gone far—the Show was out at Jamhuri
Park, some miles away on the edge of town—when
he spoke up. "I say, Stephanie, I'm awfully sorry
about the other night. I honestly didn't know the
score, or I'd have come to the rescue."

"What *is* the score?" I asked, unhelpfully.

"Oh Lor', " he rubbed his chin. "Now I've really put my foot in it."

"For God's sake," I exclaimed, rather loudly because I was as nervous as he was. "Life's too short. You asked Gillian what all the fuss was about, and Gillian said . . . ?"

"I rather gathered . . . Well, I mean people *think* . . . At least according to Gillian they think—that your mother's death may not, well, have been an accident." He stopped wretchedly, but I did not prompt. "That your father may have had a hand in it."

So now it was out—in words, in the open. I suppose it had occurred to me the night before, but I couldn't bring myself to confront it. "Any particular theories?" I asked acidly.

"The business with the hat and the pipe, for one thing . . . " he hesitated.

"Go ahead. You know more than I do."

"According to Gillian they found his hat and pipe in or near the car, but absolutely no other trace, like blood or anything. And they had sniffing dogs and hundreds of people beating the bush for days. So it did rather look as though those things were left there deliberately to mislead."

"Then why did they go to all that trouble searching if it was so obvious?" I threw out.

Richard shrugged. "They had to be sure. But I'm honestly not qualified to have an opinion. Gillian's the only one I've talked to and she gets it from hear-say."

"Does Gillian think he did it?"

"I'm afraid she does." And so do her parents, I thought, and so does the cigar-smoking Mrs. Munson. And so, probably, does Kassim Salim, although I couldn't be sure of that. "I say," Richard began again a couple of roundabouts later, "re Gillian. I'm a mite concerned in that department."

"Not the gin?" It was an attempt at frivolity.

"You're jolly observant." He was deadly serious. "I don't know if you could have a word. She ignores my advice. It's absolutely the worst thing if you're pregnant. All the books say so."

"I'll try," I promised. So that was what we were about. He went on morosely, "You know what they say about these Happy Valley Settler types—sex, booze, dope, you name it."

"Oh, but not Gillian," I said.

He shook his head slowly. "She just doesn't have enough to do."

Poor Gillian, poor Richard, I said to myself.

We passed the racecourse and the war memorial and joined a slow-moving line of Show-bound vehicles. "Can I ask you a businessy question?" He brightened as I explained about our house and how the Santorettis had bought it from the bank. "Is there any way to find out what happened?" He promised to look into it.

We were to meet 'Gillian and co.' in the Members'

Enclosure. Richard had mentioned that his father-in-law was a Governor-for-life of the Show but when I asked him what that meant he wasn't sure. One of the duties, it seemed to me, was to preen himself before assorted VIPs resplendent in a bottle-green blazer with gold buttons and a special badge—for that is what he was doing when we found them. The three of them—Gillian and her mother were in frocks and pretty hats—made me feel like something that had crawled in under the fence. I'd have been happier in the surrounding bleachers with the throngs of regular Kenyans of all shades, or even among the tribal dancers who were massing at one end of the arena with shields and spears and feathery headdresses, blowing weird warm-up notes on twisted horns to the patter and thud of drums.

Jeans notwithstanding, I was much more at ease than at the dinner the week before. My role, obvious then to all but me, was now clear: I was the piteous left-over in a scandalous murder.

The excitement of the moment was that Mrs. Munson's headman's goats had won second prize in the Nubian milk category and she was off somewhere sharing in the glory. Returning she reiterated her insistence that I come up and stay at Ravine, and this time I didn't discourage the idea, nor make the mistake of asking about my mother's grave, nor of mentioning my intent to track down Samweli, our former houseboy. Relief all round. Then President Kenyatta entered the arena, toured full circle standing in the back of a Land Rover, and proceeded to review an honor guard drawn up in the center. This done, the presidential party was ushered past us into the presidential box and the captain of the guard ordered the Retreat: "Your Excellency, may I have your permission to march off?"

A wave of the celebrated fly-whisk, then clear, low and deliberate, "Permission granted."

As we settled down to the tribal dancing, I couldn't help thinking of that time ten years ago when this same fly-whisk had waved off my parents to oblivion and myself to exile in Canada, and for the first time I really did have the feeling that perhaps I had come home.

❧

Monday morning I called in sick to the school. Heather, my co-assistant, took the message so that I didn't have to sound sick, which I'm not good at. I'd made enquiries and found that the place to go to forage in old newspapers was the basement of the McMillan Library, downtown. It turned out to be a pleasant stone-columned, jacaranda-shrouded mausoleum of a building lurking behind the Bank of Baroda. A spiral staircase hewn in stone—such as one might expect in a medieval castle but not in the tropics—led to a dimly lit subterranean chamber, its shelves stuffed with yellowing, acrid bundles. I was the sole occupant.

Once I'd got the hang of the system, I found the relevant alcove fairly quickly and carried a bundle of ten-year-old *Standard*s to a table where there was light and a chair. One thing that puzzled me was the ten-day interval—according to Wellington's clippings—between my mother's death and her funeral at Ravine. I guessed there might have been an inquest. I found more than I'd bargained for, almost at once.

In the paper of Monday, April 15th, Easter Monday, on an inside page devoted to Safari news, was a neatly-razored excision. With trembling fingers—corny, yes, but so true—I matched my talisman to the gap. A perfect fit. And in that same beautiful moment it occurred to me why Wellington had not included anything from Monday's *Standard* in his collection: he, too, had used the McMillan Library. Without stopping to check for an accompanying story, or even read the caption, I corkscrewed back up the stairs.

Earlier, at the desk, the librarian had told me to sign in before going down. Now I pounced on the sign-in book and started reading backwards. W.W. Oloo was on the previous page in neat, round script. I kept going: one week, two weeks, three weeks, a month, two months. Feverish anticipation grudgingly yielded to resignation. I wasn't even sure what I was looking for. Surely I didn't expect to see my father's name writ large for the world to note. Besides, it was unlikely that anyone who came to vandalize library property would sign in at all. Easy enough to slip downstairs when the librarian's back was turned; or, if necessary, make up a name. I returned to the stacks.

The caption under the excised photo read as follows: "Car number 48, the Humber Super Snipe of Mr. and Mrs. Dick Duncan, where it plunged off the road near Ena Bridge late Friday night. Mrs. Duncan was killed, her husband is still missing." The photo credit read, A.N. Shah. I noted down the name. No other mention of the accident occurred in Monday's paper.

I was right about the inquest. According to a small notice which appeared the following Saturday on a local news page, "An inquest was held before District Magistrate C.C.X. de Souza into the death on Friday, April 12th, near Embu of Mrs. Helen Duncan of Nairobi. A verdict of accidental death was returned. There was no postmortem."

The librarian informed me that they did not keep the other English-language newspapers, the *Standard* being the paper of record. It was suggested I try the offices of the publications themselves. This, I decided, was a job for Wellington Waki Oloo. I had another job for him, too. The problem was how to find him. I had the afternoon free and didn't want to wait until Friday.

CHAPTER ELEVEN

Funny thing: I went to Wellington Waki Oloo's
'office,' found the door open, and walked in. The
place was deserted except for three cats which
showed up when I called *"Hodi! Hodi!"*—Swahili for
'Hi, I'm here! Can I come in!' Only I was already in.
The cats soon lost interest and slunk off, so I sat
down at the bar and wondered what to do. Ten minutes later I was still wondering when in came the
youth I had seen before. He looked as though he'd
been running but was trying not to let it show. *"Jambo,"* I said. No response. He had in his hand a
rag, and drifted around applying it here and there
to random surfaces. "Excuse me, where can I find
Mr. Oloo?" Perhaps he was deaf. "I was here on Friday with Mr. Oloo. Do you know where he is now?"
On Friday he'd spoken English. I marshalled some
Swahili. *"Bwana Oloo iko wapi?"*

"Sijui." I don't know; or more pointedly, you are
wasting your time here. I took the hint.

Wandering down the hill to the Y, I contemplated
the elusive Mr. Oloo, who had dropped, or been
dropped, so generously into my lap. What was going
through his mind about all this? What could he
know about the world my parents moved in? It
struck me that had anyone really wanted to help me

in my quest they'd have hired almost any of the private detectives that walked the streets of Nairobi before they hired Wellington Waki Oloo. The man was a joke. His 'office,' his 'classified sources of information,' his very name. Like most people who are handed something for nothing, I wanted more and better. I sat in my room feeling sorry for myself until my name crackled over the p.a. system. Waiting for me in the lobby, cherubic smile unfazed by the sternly disapproving frown of the guardian matron, was Wellington Waki Oloo.

"I have only to wish, and you are here," I told him when we were out of earshot. I suppose I felt guilty. "It's quite uncanny."

"I have my beeper."

"Oh yes?" I hadn't noticed.

"The African model."

"Aha." I think I know what he meant: a sort of telepathy which has all but died out in more automated societies. However, I had a shrewd suspicion that, in this instance, the telephone had played its part.

Wellington readily fell in with my plan to hunt up Mugwe, our old cook, and soon we were speeding (a relative term) out of town along the airport road armed with the directions given me by Signor Santoretti. We passed the airport turnoff and continued in the direction of Mombasa through grassy, flat country. "It is very far." He glanced worriedly at the petrol gauge which was teetering around empty, and gave it a bang with his fist. At last we reached our turnoff and proceeded for a mile along a dead straight track. Looking back I could see a grey plume of dust settling in our wake. Wellington sneezed. "Black cotton soil. It is good to come before the rains."

I asked him when the rains were expected.

He leaned out of the window and looked intently at the edge of the road. "Not yet," he said. "When the rain is coming the white ants know and a few days before little mounds are seen, pushing up, so they are ready to come out when the time comes."

There were the 'long rains' and the 'short rains,' I recalled, subjects of intense and continual speculation on the farm; one lot fell in the autumn—May/June in Kenya—the other in the spring, around October, but which was which I'd forgotten. Our destination seemed to be a sort of oasis of trees and buildings rising out of the plain, the only habitat in sight. A single line looped towards it, carrying power I presume since Santoretti had told me the house was not on the phone. We pulled up by a high chain-link fence into which was set a gate secured by padlocks. I got out. A sultry stillness enfolded the place which comprised some broken-down shacks, a water tank, and a couple of pickup trucks, with here and there among the vegetation a splash of natural color.

I signalled Wellington who pipped the horn. The next moment a noise like the biblical rushing mighty wind assailed my ears. I spun round in time to see a ton of dogflesh hit the wire mesh, straining it to bursting; at least a dozen animals, howling in a most unwelcoming way. I'm not that fond of dogs, so I got back into the VW. Nor, apparently, was Wellington: he was winding up the windows. We looked at the dogs and the dogs glared at us, until at last they parted to let a man through. The man was small and grizzled, burned brown, and the dogs watched his every move. Even as I approached the fence, it was him they watched. His response to my explanatory patter was to start unlocking the gate. When the last lock was off and Wellington sneaked a foot out of the car, an angry current rippled through the pack. I signalled to him to stay put and stuck close to the man as we made for one of the huts.

A couple of favored creatures were allowed inside, but even these were left behind in a sort of scullery as the old man bustled down a dark passage and I followed. A meaty smell tainted the air, suggesting dogfood, but even so I wasn't prepared for the sight that met my eyes when he pushed open a door. The room had obviously been a bedroom, perhaps still was, because a four-poster nearly filled it. Across the counterpane was stretched—like strands of thick, yellowing hair—spaghetti; drying, I suppose. And hanging over it—all shapes and sizes dangling from the cross-beams—salami. The man patted the bedspread where the pillow was. "My wife," he said, affectionately.

My God, I thought, according to Santoretti she'd been dead ten years.

Without waiting for my response, which was slow in coming, my host darted around the bed and ducked through a far door, gesturing me to stay put. Soon I heard him calling, and the excited snapping and barking of the dogs. Stay put I did. Wait till I tell Yvonne about this, I thought. As an ancient Roman once said, in Latin, "Always something new out of Africa."

When Mugwe made his appearance it was almost anticlimactic. He stood in the doorway blinking at me through the salami. I don't think he had the faintest idea who I was. "Mugwe, *habari ya siku nyingi?*" I said, drawing out the last word. "How have you been these many days?"

"*Memsab 'dogo?*" Little Madame? His face had shrivelled, his hair was completely grey.

"Yes, it's me. Stephanie."

He walked around the bed like a man who dares not blink in case a vision dissolves. It wasn't till we had shaken hands for some time and hard that he satisfied himself I was flesh and blood.

As we stood at the end of the bed—there was no place to sit that was pasta-free—Mugwe recalled the last time he'd seen me, the evening we had hurried in out of the rain together. He had given me supper and later the couple had come with whom I was to spend the weekend; people from the club called Sheila and Gordon Barnes. Funny, I'd completely put them out of my mind. Perhaps it was they who put me on the plane for Canada. Mr. Barnes had returned that Saturday, told Mugwe about the accident and asked him to take charge of the house. Samweli, who had been on leave, had journeyed back from Ravine on the Monday, having heard the news on the radio. It was Mugwe's opinion that my father had been carried off and eaten by a leopard. His maternal grandmother, who lived near the mountain, had suffered this fate, having been dragged from her hut in broad daylight. Not a trace had been found of her, just paw-marks in the dust.

Had Mugwe noticed anything ūnusual at home in the weeks before the Safari? I asked. He thought for a little before saying, sadly, that things were "not as before." What had seemed to be most on my parents' minds? "Safari, Safari, Safari," he replied. Many weekends they had spent away in the car, and many evenings at the club. But was that unusual? I asked; ever since I could remember they'd spent all their spare time between Christmas and Easter getting ready for the big rally, driving over the route, charting it in detail. I'd rather resented never being allowed to go. "Too risky," they'd say.

It was different this time, Mugwe insisted; but in the face of all my cajoling, he wouldn't or couldn't be specific, as a last resort suggesting I ask Samweli. "Samweli *najua*," he said. Samweli knows. Why Samweli and not him? Because a man had come to visit Samweli one day, before the Italian had moved in. The man, whom Mugwe did not know, had come to the servants' quarters. He had gone to Samweli's half and Mugwe had heard them talking. It was odd for a European to visit the servants' quarters. Even Bwana Duncan had never done this.

What did they talk about? I wanted to know. But Mugwe knew only that they talked; and that afterwards Samweli had been "very quiet." "Samweli *najua*," he repeated with growing assurance. And Samweli, as far as he knew, was back at his *shamba* near Ravine. Mugwe hadn't seen him since the wife of the Italian had chased them both away.

I sensed that the old cook was restless; perhaps after too many questions. But no, he protested, it was just that it was time to prepare the food. I expressed surprise; it was only four o'clock in the afternoon; how many was he cooking for?

Fifteen, he replied wearily.

"I saw only the old Italian."

Not people, dogs, he explained. "I am a cook for dogs."

We shook hands and I promised rashly to come again, often. The old Italian stepped in—I think he'd been waiting in the passage—and led me to the gate. This time we were not serenaded by the pack. I could hear them yelping in the distance; possibly salivating at the prospect of the morsels their European-trained chef was about to serve up.

On the drive back I told Wellington that I'd like to go over the Safari course myself, "at least the bit around Mount Kenya."

"The Safari course?" He sounded alarmed.

"Whatever became of my parents, it's all bound up

with the Safari. I've got to get into my thick head exactly what was happening. But don't worry, I won't ask *you* to drive me. I know someone with exactly the right car."

He looked a bit hurt, banged the petrol gauge a few times, smiled and put his foot down. The VW didn't exactly leap forward, though Wellington did, behind the wheel. "This *gari*," he boasted, "it is very good with mud."

CHAPTER TWELVE

Y vonne turned up after supper looking disgust-
ingly happy. I asked her why. "I can't talk about it
till it's over," she smirked. "It's bad karma for me to
boast about an affair."

"Jeez," I said. "Do you mind if I throw up?" I needed her for a scheme I was hatching and foresaw com-
plications. "By the way, are you free next weekend?"

Just as I feared. "Next weekend," she said dreami-
ly. "Oh well, I suppose I'll have to tell you. I'm flying
down to the coast for the weekend. Sorry."

"That good? Wow." Bloody hell, I thought. I wasn't
sure I could manage Kassim alone.

As it turned out I didn't even have to ask him. He
phoned me at the school next day. "How about coming for a spin this weekend, Stephanie? I'll show you
some of the sights." (Miss Duncan no longer, please
note.)

"Love to. Just three conditions. We take the Humber. We go round Mount Kenya. And I ask a friend."

He hesitated. "If you insist. We can't do it in a day,
not in the Humber. You realize that? We'll have to
spend a night en route."

"How about Embu?"

"There's a nice inn at Embu, actually. We'll have to be up with the sun, though, to make it comfortably."

"Fine with me." I hung up. I was pretty sure now who had employed Wellington.

"Stephanie," Miss Hickle poked her head out of her office, "may I suggest that you arrange your assignations in your own time from now on. We do not run a dating service here." I stuck out my tongue at the closing door. Heather giggled.

In the hour before dawn a strange ritual is enacted on the streets of Nairobi. Gaudily-clad, space-helmeted men stride resolutely home like creatures from another planet escaping the light of mortal day. They go armed. It is the changing of the watch.

We nosed along through the drowsy city. Yvonne, in the back seat, had already nodded off. Predictably, her weekend at the coast had fallen through and she had graciously consented to accompany me on the Mount Kenya trip; probably on the chance of another go at Kassim. It was too early for conversation, so I sat back, watching lorry-loads of vegetables trundling precariously past bound for the city markets and enjoying the movement of the car in Kassim's skillful hands. Less than an hour out of town we stopped at a country inn for breakfast; but the best that could be had so early was tea and biscuits. While the kettle was boiling, Kassim and I strolled across a dewy lawn to look at some rather spectacular waterfalls, leaving Yvonne to sleep.

"I want a crash course in the Safari," I said.

"Not exactly, I trust."

I bit my lip. We were off to a great start. "I'd like to see—where it happened. Do you think you could find the spot?"

"I don't know. I was away at the time. But we'll give it a good try."

"We could ask around. Surely someone would re-member."

"We'll find it, don't worry." He briefly held my arm, then turned to walk back. I shivered. The cool greenness of the place was wonderfully soothing, with the background rush of the falls plunging sixty feet in a column of spray. A bridge spanned the river directly above them; I think we had driven over on it. As I watched, a red car sped across, going much too fast. It seemed incongruous.

Yvonne appeared as we were sipping the strong tea in a sort of glassed-in balcony overlooking a gar-den. "Just look at the lovebirds." She stood, hands on hips, the picture of indignation. For some reason I started apologizing. Kassim sat back, amused. Adding to the effect, a couple of maribou storks sauntered up behind her, peering accusingly at us with solemn hangdog attitudes, long beaks propped against their breasts. Kassim threw them a biscuit. When we set off again I surrendered the front seat.

"I'm warning you," Kassim looked over his shoulder at me, "You may get more than you bargained for."

"Oh?"

"The met man forecasts rain."

" 'The chocolate pudding safari.' Ideal." Kassim glanced back again, eyebrows raised. "Oh, I've done my homework." I had too. I'd read up all I could on that particular Safari in those back copies of the *Standard*. "Are *you* an 'old man of the mud'?"

"My goodness, those sportswriters. Perhaps we'll find out." He explained to Yvonne, who was completely in the dark.

The Humber wound its way steadily into the heart of Kikuyuland towards the invisible mountaintop. It moved like a sage black bird, with Kassim, an integral part, practically crowing at the wheel. In the back seat I alternately dozed and looked out of the window at the passing scene: the pervasive redness of the soil, the dusty scrub, the herds of multicolored goats and gaunt hump-backed cows with their ragged little attendants, the occasional row of tin *dukas* or shops, the simple homesteads with here and there a modern brick villa or a church; above all the people, so many of them, going about their business.

The road dipped and rose, but mostly rose. We passed a couple of bigger towns clustered around hilltops before stopping at Nanyuki for lunch because Yvonne wanted to have a drink served to her across the Equator. She'd heard that the bar at one of the hotels was precisely on the line. A lemonade was duly handed over and she scribbled a postcard home.

It was here at Nanyuki, Kassim told us, that we joined the Safari route. That particular year, he recalled, the cars had been sent up to Kampala through the Nandi Hills and Kakamega and had been brought back from Uganda via Kapenguria, Tambach, Nakuru and Thomson's Falls, and across the top end of the Aberdares into Nanyuki.

I asked him when he'd last competed.

"Gosh, it's been ten years; no, eleven."

"So why did you chuck it in?" Yvonne wanted to know.

"If it's not something you want to do more than anything else, then there's no point. Nothing's casual about it. You don't just get in a car and drive any more than you run a marathon because you think it might be fun." He added, "I suppose, for me, the heart went out of it."

"Did you ever do this stretch around the mountain?"

"Many times. They usually manage to fit it in in some shape or form. You'll see why later on."

Ten years ago, Kassim pointed out, the blacktop ended at Nanyuki. Now it extended all the way round the northern slopes of Mount Kenya as far as Meru to the northeast. The mountain today was still shrouded in cloud. For some time I'd felt tension building in the atmosphere as the sky turned a progressively darker grey. We heard sporadic thunder. Yvonne complained of a headache. Probably a touch of altitude. We were quite high. Then big dabs of water hit the windscreen and rattled against the roof. Kassim slowed our speed and switched on the headlights, peering ahead at the tarmac, which shone like a choppy sea. Visibility was down to about fifty yards, but the road was straight and traffic by this time was light so we kept on. Soon, however, I could scarcely see the silver squirrel mounted atop the radiator grill: the wipers had no impact at all. It was as if we were sitting under a waterfall, hemmed in by falling water, deafened by it. Still, the Humber crept on. I looked at Yvonne. Her eyes were shut tight. We stopped. "Better let this blow over," Kassim said cheerfully.

"Shouldn't we pull onto the shoulder?" We were in the middle of the road.

"No," Kassim shouted above the din, "if it's soft, this beast takes a lot of pushing. A ton and a half of steel. Anyone moving out there is either blind or suicidal."

I sat back. It was really quite cozy. Ten years ago my parents had passed this way. By my calculations it would have been dark already, probably raining. They'd have been more than twenty-four hours on the road by now. The horrendous conditions already had knocked out half the field, including some world-class drivers, yet my parents were still plugging along. I felt an irrational thrill of pride, and wondered who had been driving and who navigating.

After ten minutes the rain let up sufficiently for us to continue. By the time we reached Meru town it had stopped. I liked the look of Meru. The township was run of the mill, but the green of the surrounding forest was truly sparkling after the rain and the place exuded a wholesome air. Even the people seemed better-disposed towards us. Kassim—winking—said it was because Europeans had never managed to grab the land, which was fertile and well-watered, but ridgy.

On the way out of town we stopped at the pub because Yvonne had to answer a call of nature; and it was just as well that we did. Indeed, had we not, I might still not know the truth about my parents. So I owe Yvonne a lot, and, in spite of what transpired later, still think of her with gratitude.

The Pig and Whistle at Meru is a comfortably decaying spread of thatched rondavals with wide verandahs set off by lush lawns, purple jacarandas and orange flame trees. Naturalists, Kassim assured me, come here for the butterflies; also the odd tourist bound for Meru National Park with its lion, cheetah, rhino, buffalo, leopard, elephant, lesser kudu, crocodile and reticulated giraffe. While Yvonne dashed in to do her business, we sat out front in the Humber watching the white ants, lured by the rain, come pouring out of their holes in the ground flapping their feeble wings just as Wellington had predicted. "The dance of death," said Kassim. A cat crouched in the grass, gorging itself on the curling, glistening bodies. "Some people fry them. Very nutritious, I'm told."

Though the afternoon was still young, he seemed anxious to press on, reckoning to allow three hours minimum for the Meru to Embu stretch; there were ninety-nine hairpin bends in as many miles on loose murram with steep drops down the side. I suggested he not repeat this to Yvonne. "So you see why it was so beloved of the Safari organizers: it sorted out the sheep from the goats."

Only, in the Safari in question, as I pointed out,

the sheep and the goats had already been sorted; only the goats were left.

"Bit of bad luck there, actually. As I recall, the course originally included the lower road between here and Embu, the plains road; smooth sailing all the way to Nairobi. But the rains swelled up a river which knocked out a bridge and the old hairpin section was substituted at the last minute by the Clerk of the Course." He looked towards the inn. "I say, perhaps I should just check on the roads now. No harm done, and we don't want to spend the night in the bush if we can help it." He was out of the car and striding across the spongy grass before I could comment. I followed, making a detour to observe the cat which hissed at me and was incredibly fat.

Kassim, when I found him in the dim interior, had run to ground a dishevelled European who was either Mine Host or an habitué of the place and had clearly been enjoying a nap on a sofa. "They're grading the road as far as Chuka," he was saying, "and with all the rain we've been getting, frankly I wouldn't touch it."

Kassim's reply eluded me, but the man, who had run flabbily to fat and was wearing a straw hat with the brim pulled down all the way round, grunted. "Please yourself." At the same time, over Kassim's shoulder, he fixed me with an oily grin.

I knew from my reading that Meru had been a Safari checkpoint, and it struck me that the Pig and Whistle might have been its location. So I asked the man, telling him briefly who I was. His eyes bulged, "But I stamped their card! I was control officer. My heavens, what a night to remember! They straggled in till all hours, limping and coughing and caked in mud—the cars, I mean; the place looked like an earthquake evacuation center, people dossed down everywhichwhere. You never saw such a sight. Kept the control open till first light, we did. Of course it was hopeless; most of them were time-barred, poor darlings."

"But surely not my parents," I put in quickly. Yvonne had joined us and I sensed Kassim's impatience to be off. "Did anything strike you particularly? Who was driving?"

"I'm almost sure it was your father, because your mother brought over the card. We chatted a bit. Nothing seemed amiss, though naturally everyone was tense. The usual questions, 'Who're the leaders? How's it up front?' They would stay here quite often on their recces, specially that year, spent a lot of time up this way did your parents, so I got to know them a teeny bit. Charming people. Such a loss. Of course I told the police everything at the time." He saw us to the door. I was last out. He stared at me and shook his head so that his chins wobbled, "Knew I'd seen you somewhere. Never forget a face."

"Who was *that*?" I asked as we pulled away. I was back in the front seat. "The innkeeper?"

"No, no. He lives there—with his boyfriend. I think he was P.W.D. up here—Public Works Department—

or was it Education? When he retired, he just hung around, a bit of Imperial detritus you might say; one of the army of Safari volunteers. I have a specially fond memory of him, from when he let one of his cronies, whom I'd overtaken, start out ahead of me at his control. I had to eat the chap's dust half way round the mountain."

"Do you think he remembered? He told me he never forgets a face."

"Depends on the face." We crossed a bridge and turned sharply left. "Slight change of route," Kassim announced. He explained that since the road that hugged the mountain was being graded—the murram scraped from the sides into the middle—it would be a quagmire after the rain. He was not about to sink his precious car into a muddy grave for nothing. So we would take the plains road and get back onto the mountain road at Chuka. There was a connecting road he knew about.

My parents had passed through the Chuka control; that was where I wanted to go. "What exactly does 'time-barred' mean?" I asked.

"You're racing against the clock, right? There's a time limit set between control points. Each minute you're late counts a point against you. If your lateness points add up to more than the total allowed overall, you're time-barred and have to drop out. Simple as that. If the going is particularly tough and most of the field is barred, the Clerk of the Course can extend lateness time. That's how your parents were still in the race: maximum lateness was extended—probably from four hours to six on the northern leg, something like that. They were hanging on by the skin of their teeth, which means a hell of a lot of pressure."

"Yet they had time to chat with old what's-his-name back there?"

"Only because Meru was a designated rest stop as well as being a control point. They had a fifteen-minute wait in any case. There are rest stops every two or three hundred miles."

"So Chuka wasn't a rest stop?"

"Chuka was just in and out. Get your route card stamped and go."

Chuka was a few buildings clinging to the side of a hill in a lush, foresty area. We had turned off the plains road just after a bridge, which, according to Kassim, had been washed out and caused the route change. It was an easy run up to Chuka on a narrow connecting road.

"Let's think now, the checkpoint at Chuka, I seem to remember, was the school." Kassim pondered aloud. We made a right—the signpost pointing back towards Meru—and after a few hundred yards pulled into a small compound. CHUKA FULL PRIMARY SCHOOL, a board announced. I jumped out and tried the door. Locked. I walked round the back peering in at the windows. It was Saturday afternoon; the place was deserted.

"Can I help you?" A man had come out of a smaller building and was walking towards me. He seemed young and friendly, and he'd spoken English.

"Well, perhaps. Do you know if the school here is ever used as a control point in the Safari Rally?"

"Oh yes," he said. "Many times."

"Are you sure?" His confidence startled me. Had he understood?

"Even I myself am headmaster."

"Oh, I'm sorry. I mean, I see." I blushed. He certainly wasn't old enough to have been headmaster in my parents' day. "Well, thanks." I backed away.

"Excuse me, this is your car?"

"No, actually, it's a friend's."

"Humbah Supah Sinipe." He stared at it. "Excuse me, you will take tea with me? Also your friend?" (Yvonne was stretched out in the back, invisible.)

"We really must be pushing on, thank you." Smoke was drifting enticingly from the chimney of his house. "Have to make Embu before dark."

"Go, but carefully." He stood watching, rather forlornly, as we took off. I guessed he was lonely.

We were heading for Ena and the last checkpoint my parents had passed through together and alive. We were traveling the same road they had traveled in almost the same car. I'd been promised the hairpin bends they'd negotiated, and hairpin bends I got. The road was narrow and slippery, the drop to our left terrifying. Yvonne moaned gently in the back. We met two cars and a bus and had to reverse into a lay-by so the bus could squeeze past. Kassim did it in forty minutes because, as he put it, he was rusty. In the old days he'd have shaved that by ten.

Normally drivers would be told the route a couple of months ahead of time. They would scrutinize it section by section noting every bridge, every awkward bend, what speeds to average, where to stop for petrol. Recce runs, Kassim called them (for reconnaissance); though my parents, as he pointed out, might have been rusty on this stretch too, expecting, as they did, the plains road. And, an added hazard, they were doing it at night.

The rain began again as we drove into Ena, not as fiercely as before but with drenching steadiness. Ena was hardly bigger than Chuka and boasted a fair-sized bridge. It was just before this bridge, at a small health center, that the control point had been established. Here the plains road rejoined the mountain road and the Safari got back on course.

"So this was just an in-and-out control as well?" I asked.

"Yes," he pointed. "A table would be set up over there under the eaves manned by two or three officials. Drivers would pull in here, jump out—or more likely the navigator would jump out—get their card stamped and zoom off again. If there was any little thing that needed doing, like wiping the headlights, they might do that."

We sat in the car with the drip drip, trickle trickle of the rain all around us and contemplated the dreary scene. "Where are all the people?" I asked. "Doesn't anyone live around here?"

"Oh yes, a lot of people. Only they have more sense

than us. They're snug at home around the fire. You'd be surprised at the crowds that show up when the Safari goes through."

"Even at midnight?"

"Even at midnight." He painted the scene for us:

Headlights glinting way off along the mountain, coming nearer, the officials around their hurricane lamp swiping distractedly at moths, the District Officer's Land Rover parked over there, the excitement rippling through the throngs of children and adults when a car shoots up the road and squeals to a halt, a couple of policemen trying to keep order, perhaps friends coming forward with freshly-made samosas *or cups of tea, a ham radio operator raising Nairobi or the next town down the line, the shouted questions* . . .

"I'd like to track down whoever was in charge here," I said.

"They were usually local people. Perhaps tomorrow, at Embu?" Kassim slipped the car into second gear and we rattled across the bridge. "It's macadam now, but in those days this road was still dirt. All the same, after the nightmare she'd come through, it's hard to understand . . . " His voice petered out. "I mean, mud was her element. Dick liked the long-haul fast bits."

True, after what we'd come through the road seemed straightforward, the curves and the drops unspectacular. We passed a small turn-off on the mountainside and Kassim slowed down. "It was somewhere along here." He veered across the road and pulled up on the right-hand shoulder. We all leaned over to look out. A red car swished by, barreling south.

CHAPTER FOURTEEN

We stood in the rain, Kassim, Yvonne, myself, peering into a deep gorge, like birdwatchers. No weathered chassis, nothing but greenery and an odd protruding boulder met our gaze. A raw mist claimed everything, its tentacles reaching down the mountainside. Yvonne slipped an arm around my waist. Not that I needed comfort. I felt detached, a bystander at someone else's tragedy. It was a relief when Kassim said, "May I make a suggestion? That we come back tomorrow. It's only six or seven miles to Embu, and the rain usually holds off in the mornings. More likely to find someone to ask."

We turned off just before Embu, the district headquarters, into the grounds of the Izaak Walton Inn. The streams around were stocked with trout and the inn served as an angler's mecca, hence the name. I asked Kassim if he fished. "Deep-sea, not this sort of thing, I'm afraid." My father was an avid fisherman, I remembered. I had a vision of his green rubber waders, almost as big as me, flopped over in a cupboard at the farm. He used to fly up to a lake in the north somewhere and go out with the local tribesmen; promising—always promising—some day to take me along.

Dusk was coming on. The giant pepper trees on the lawn drooped like venerable Magi cloaked against the drizzle. We ducked in under a golden-shower that hung from the verandah roof. Kassim had made reservations and apologized for the fact that Yvonne and I would have to share: the place was full. The rooms were strung out either side of the main building, each giving onto the garden that sloped gently down, flowerbed by flowerbed, to a mountain stream. Africa overlayed by England; beguiling, indeed. The very trout in the stream had come from England, I was proudly told. As we sipped our tea in sagging leather armchairs by a log fire it was easy to forget the insubstantiality of it all.

Yvonne went for a bath and a lie-down before dinner, leaving Kassim and myself stretched out in our chairs. "Now don't get up to any hanky panky." She shook a parting finger at us. It was getting a bit hard to take.

I turned to Kassim. "What do you really think happened to my father?"

He was polishing his glasses with the silk handkerchief that dangled from the pocket of the snazzy blazer he'd donned in his room. Now he breathed on them, rubbed some more, and held them up to the firelight. "I wondered when you were going to toss that one at me."

"Do you think he's alive?"

He shook his head. "If I were you I'd put that possibility right out of my mind. Of course there'll always be rumors: that he was seen here, there or the other place. But no, to all intents and purposes he must be considered dead."

"But what could have happened? I mean it was dark, they're driving along, bushed out after thirty plus hours behind the wheel, *just* avoiding being time-barred, and they go off the edge. That much I see. By the way, didn't anyone see anything?"

"If so they didn't come forward or it would have been reported sooner."

"So we don't really know if they were both in the car at the time."

He looked surprised. "It was generally assumed, of course."

"Some people think . . . Do *you* think that he could have, say, *pushed* her over?"

Kassim thought. "I suppose he *could* have. He was in good shape physically. If they'd stopped on the very brink, for some reason. He wouldn't have had a lot of time before the next car came along. But why? It's absurd. At its crudest level, please forgive me, your mother wasn't even insured. No," he slapped his thigh, "I'll bet my entire collection that he didn't."

I believed him. "And if he'd gone over with her, could he have walked away?"

"Accidents have odd dynamics; again and again, I've seen it. In this case, as it happens, the main damage was on the driver's side. Must have bounced off a rock, or something."

"So what happened to him?" My question had a plaintive ring to it.

"I don't think we'll ever know."

We were all three whacked after our early morning start and headed for bed directly after supper. I was asleep before Yvonne had even finished brushing her teeth.

I awoke a while later: one of those slow dawnings of the mind that begin in some deep forgotten dream and swim upward through the surface of consciousness to intense clarity; the nicest way to wake up. Something was different. I lay on my back, quite still; the night felt still around me, hemmed in by the monotonous chirrup of the crickets. I turned my head: Yvonne's bed was empty.

Since I'd no idea of the time, it occurred to me that she was still cleaning her teeth; but no light shone from the adjoining bathroom. I got up and checked, just to make sure. Thoughts of Mugwe's leopard sprang to mind—the one that had removed his grandmother without a trace. But leopards don't go round opening hotel doors; especially locked doors. Yes, I *had* locked the door: it opened onto a verandah running the length of the building, along with all the other doors. And it was still locked, with the key in the lock. I was about to freak out when I remembered the other door, the one that gave onto the garden. Yvonne, unable to sleep—she'd dozed a good deal in the car—was probably sitting on our

own little balcony admiring the moonlit garden.
Yes, the key was in the door and the door was open. I
stepped out. No Yvonne.

The rain had stopped. The night was bright. The
African night never seems to get dark if you're out
in it. Somewhere a guest was snoring. Or perhaps
the watchman. Standing on the prickly matting in
bare feet and pyjamas I could see all the way to the
trees on the far bank of the stream. And above them
more trees, and far in the distance the jagged out-
line of the peak itself, a hovering ethereal presence.
I stared in wonder till a bloodcurdling shriek
pierced the stillness; a rock hyrax.

I am not Yvonne's keeper, I told myself firmly; her
life is not my business. So her weekend at the coast
falls through? So, to oblige a friend, she lets herself
be dragged around Mount Kenya, alternately bored
and petrified? So she catches a man's eye and keeps
a midnight tryst? A twinge of prurient admiration
crept into me: when, how, where, who? The guy at
the bar who spilled his drink over her? The waiter
at dinner she'd winked at? The Complete Angler
whose fish story had so entranced her? (No, he had a
wife in tow.) Her technique must be pretty good. No
doubt I'd hear all about it in the morning.

According to my watch, it was just past three. I
turned in and was getting back into bed when I
noticed something sticking under the door. An envelope. It hadn't been there five minutes earlier. I
picked it up. On it three capitals, large and black,
S.A.D. My initials. Only they weren't in the correct

order, at least not the way I'd arranged them any time recently. (What possessed my parents to put Stephanie before Adeline I'll never know; perhaps it was the vicar.) The flap was sealed, the letters—cut from a newspaper as far as I could tell—glued over it. I switched on the light, but, on second thoughts, switched it off again, ripped open the envelope and went and stood by the window.

'GOOD GIRL FOR COMING,' I read in the same roughly stuck caps. 'TELL AND TRUST NO ONE. YOU ARE BETTER OFF MINUS ME. ALL I WANT IS YOU TO KNOW TRUTH. BURN THIS. LOVE.' That was it.

My hand was on the doorknob; a more hot-blooded person would have been out there searching in the night. But logic asserted itself. The hand behind this would surely not be caught so easily; nor, on a few seconds reflection, did I want to try. Not yet, at any rate. I crawled into bed, pulled the covers up tight around my chin, and lay for a while, thinking. I must have slept, because the morning light, flooding the room, fell across Yvonne. I hadn't heard her come in.

※

Truth. It was with somewhat altered feelings from the day before that I stood again at the edge of the road looking down into the green abyss. Yvonne had elected not to come back with us to the scene of the accident, but to sun herself on the lawn at the inn; though the sun, which had indeed sparkled through breakfast, had been eclipsed by clouds, as had the mountain. Still, it wasn't the sun that drew Yvonne, I was pretty sure; though not a word about her night had she breathed, and I hadn't asked, in deference to Karma.

Kassim had rustled up two local youths who swore they knew exactly where the Humber had gone off the road, though they could scarcely have been born at the time. We watched them moving around in the undergrowth, calling animatedly to each other, till they yelled up to us and waved.

"Here we go," said Kassim, taking my arm and stepping gingerly into the bush. "Do you think you can manage?"

I disengaged myself. "Sure."

"Watch out for snakes." We clambered from rock to rock, pushing aside leaves and branches, descending in crisscross formation to lessen the steepness. Then, there it was, a hunk of twisted, rusted metal, nose down among the rocks with vegetation crawling out of it in all directions and the boys standing by like a couple of used-car salesmen ready to pitch. Kassim made a thorough inspection. "That's it all right." He kicked gently at a rear axle where a tire should have been. "They don't make them like that any more."

The boys each received something for their trouble. They accepted gravely with both hands, but made no move to leave; much too interesting to wait and see what would happen next.

They were probably disappointed. "It must have

been tough, getting her body back up," was all I could think of to say. In my mind words went round and round. Truth. All I want is you to know truth. Tell and trust no one.

Enquiries at the inn, where we lunched before driving back to Nairobi, turned up the following. The man who was control officer at the Ena Bridge checkpoint ten years back was retired and living at the coast. The police inspector in charge of the case had moved to Rhodesia, as it then was called. The presiding magistrate at the inquest had died.

CHAPTER FIFTEEN

Wellington Waki Oloo was jubilant. I hadn't been back at the Y an hour—having begged off Kassim's warm invitation to dinner, to Yvonne's disgust—when he put in an appearance. From his suit pocket he pulled a grubby, much-folded document. "This," he presented it to me, "makes very surprising reading. Please be careful however. It is the only copy." He was backing out of the door.

"Can we talk?" I pleaded.

"I am just now rushing, but later. I have someone for you to meet who will make you happy."

"Later this evening?"

"It is possible." He dashed out to his VW, parked, as usual, in the road. I had a glimpse of small faces crammed at the windows as it pulled away.

Dinner wasn't for an hour, so I went back to my room. Sitting on the bed I smoothed out the dog-eared pages fastened by a rusty paperclip. They were roughly and faintly typed, triple space, on a skittish machine, judging by the frequent dips and leaps of the letters and the odd gaps. No title appeared, and no date, merely the pencilled instruction, 'Otieno—see me on this,' scrawled above an

'Perhaps Question Time in Parliament is not normally a sportswriter's turf, but when a major international sports event like the East African Safari Rally is the issue, we beg the floor, Mr. Speaker, Sir, trusting our colleagues in the press gallery will allow us, to raise some questions of our own.

'Last week, the Hon. M.P. for Meru South asked about the hitherto unexplained disappearance of a competitor on the Mount Kenya section of the Safari already nearly three months ago. The Hon. Assistant Minister for Home Affairs responded in a vague and defensive way and the matter sank without a trace.

'Our own enquiries of the police have similarly been routed around the bush, in the shape of blank-faced No Comments.

'So our question is: What's going on? As a host country of the Safari, surely we have a duty to the international sports community to protect drivers and other sportsmen when they compete in our country, or risk becoming a laughingstock in the eyes of the sporting world with the danger that the rally itself will be relegated to the ranks of a local free-for-all.

'Was—as the Member for Meru South implied—this unfortunate driver indeed kidnapped by *shifta* or some other group? One thing is sure: as long as the public is not told the truth, the rumor-mills will be working overtime. So let the truth be told.

'We have done our own little bit of sleuthing and

come up with some interesting anomalies which we call upon the authorities to address. But first, the facts as known to the public at large:

'On the night of Friday, April 12th, between Ena Bridge and Embu, car number 48, a Humber Super Snipe driven by Mr. and Mrs. Dick Duncan of Nairobi, plunged off the road into a ravine. Mrs. Duncan was trapped behind the wheel and crushed to death. An inquest brought in a verdict of accidental death. Her husband simply vanished. He has not been seen since.

'Anomaly number one: car number 48 was variously reported at Ena Bridge control to be "looking good" and to have sustained "a bad bash right front" which had knocked out a headlamp. No one can be found at Chuka, or at Meru, the two previous checkpoints, who noticed this damage. How did it happen?

'Anomaly number two: the record shows that the position of car 48 was different at Ena Bridge than it was at Chuka, the previous checkpoint, *by three cars.* In other words, three cars had passed it. Anyone who knows that stretch of road knows how hard it is to overtake, let alone do so without being seen. Yet not one of the six people in those cars recalls passing any other car on that stretch. So it looks as though, for reasons unknown, car 48 pulled right off the road. Why?

'Anomaly number three: between Chuka and Ena Bridge car number 48 lost 15 lateness points, points it could ill afford. None of the surviving cars lost any lateness points at all on that comparatively short section. What took car 48 so long?

'The sooner the authorities make public the extent of their investigations, the sooner the mystery of unfortunate car 48 will be laid to rest, and the sooner confidence will be restored in what is becoming one of the world's major sporting events.'

The mystery of car 48. The words took up a sort of ghostly residence in my mind. The need to talk to someone became overpowering, to share with them these few paragraphs typed ten years ago by unknown hands that so uncannily mirrored the questions on my mind today and showed that at least one person had troubled to delve intelligently into the fate of my parents. I went in search of Yvonne. She wasn't in her room. She didn't appear at supper.

After supper I hung around the lobby hoping that Wellington would show up and when he didn't I felt resentful. A visit to Club Jacaranda crossed my mind, but I managed to suppress the impulse. Lying in bed, my thoughts hovered back and forth over the road between Chuka and Ena Bridge—the road we had been on only yesterday. What, I wondered, had befallen my parents on that stretch of road? Pondering, I must have drowsed off, because I woke up to a rattling sound like hailstones against a window pane. Foggily, I pulled back the curtain, and there, beyond the hibiscus hedge, teeth gleaming in the light of the parking lot, stood Wellington. In seconds

I had pulled on some clothes and was waiting impatiently as the night guard fumbled with the lock to let me out.

Wellington was sitting under the bombax tree chatting to the old watchman. He got up when he saw me and we converged on his car. "So you know the old man?" I asked.

"He's my home boy, that one. In this business we must be friends with so many watchmen. We never know when we will need their services. It is very expensive. This old man, for instance, pointed out to me your window."

I think I blushed. So the spying was mutual. "But our guard at the Y; not helpful?"

"That one is incorruptible, or too expensive. I'm not sure which."

I returned the precious document.

"We are going now to his house," Wellington threw out. "Otieno's. He has agreed to answer all your questions."

I felt like hugging Wellington there and then as we drove along Uhuru Highway, formerly Princess Elizabeth Way. "Tell me about him."

"He's just a reporter. At that time working for the *Sunday Star*, now defunct. He wrote a column called 'Sporting Chance' with other sportswriters. This particular column," he patted his jacket where he'd stowed it, "was never printed."

"Oh?" I felt let down.

"All questions must be addressed to him."

"He's still a sportswriter?"

"He is."

"And how did you find him?"

"In a manner of speaking, he found me. He is, to a certain extent, family." He added apologetically, "And women talk."

"Well, thank goodness." I filled him in on our 'mock Safari' around the mountain and considered and rejected the idea of showing him my night letter which, instructions notwithstanding, I couldn't bring myself to destroy.

Our destination was a tomblike housing project stuck out on the flat southwestern edge of town, a bunch of multi-story buildings juxtaposed at odd angles in a bed of concrete. It could have been any upended slum in North America. Even the graffiti were in English. We parked in a lot where more than one car, I noticed, had been stripped and plundered, and walked a couple of empty blocks where the only sounds were the faint blare of radios and our own footfall. In the brightness of the night it didn't matter that most of the streetlights were out.

Otieno lived on the sixth floor of one of these high-rises. He'd been expecting us, for how long I dared not think. He and Wellington had a language in common other than English and Swahili, and, during a whispered exchange—I gathered there were people asleep in other rooms—I was able to observe him; a handsome man of perhaps thirty, with a jutting brow and the physique of a boxer; the sort it is hard not to like because they exude frankness.

We sat down in some armchairs and he got straight to business. "I am the one who is always interviewing, so now I'll relax and let you do all the work." He seemed well-briefed as to who I was and what I was up to, so I started by asking why that particular column had been spiked.

"You saw what was written, 'Otieno see me on this.' Well, I went to see him. His name was Mashan Shah, a very respected journalist in Kenya but of the old school, you understand. In fact they had pulled him out of retirement to make him editor of the *Sunday Star*, and it was he who gave me my first job, so I musn't be too tough on the old boy.

"What happened was that he'd received word back as a result of my enquiries that I was writing about this mysterious accident. And it was clear to me from what he said that pressure had been brought to bear on him not to run my piece."

A young, sleepy-looking woman had entered with a tray. She put it down on a low table and began to set out cups and saucers and pour tea. Silently and shyly she handed us each a cup and left the room.

"Who brought this pressure?" I asked. "Did you ever find out?"

"Oh yes, it came out in the end. I was very indignant, threatening to resign and so on; my first brush with censorship." He smiled. "One gets older and less principled. He had to calm me with the truth. It was the owners, it turned out. You see the *Star* was sort of an experiment. The Kenya press

108

was nearly all foreign-owned, so after *Uhuru* some businessmen got together and started it as a locally-owned, so-called multi-racial, paper; a political ploy, really, I see now. Anyway, it never got enough ads to get off the ground. You can buy a lot of things, but not, it seems, a multi-racial society."

"But what could they possibly object to in your story?"

"It was felt that the more the thing was played up, the more damage it would do internationally to the Safari image. And the government was touchy for another reason too: the failure to crack this case made it look as though they weren't really in control. There was a lot of sabre-sharpening going on in Somalia, don't forget: they were going to reclaim their 'lost territory,' the supposedly oil-rich Northern Frontier District. The *shifta* were still a factor."

"Who were these owners?"

"There were three. The Three Wise Men, we used to call them. Sayed Ali Malombo was African, a contractor down at the coast; the European was Sir Isaac Bennett of Bennett Overseas Trading; and the Asian was a big fish in Nairobi real estate, Kassim Salim, an Ismaili."

I looked at Wellington. He seemed as surprised as I was at the last name. "Not the Kassim Salim who was a rally driver?"

"Possibly. I hear he had quite a collection of old cars. In fact, you are jogging my memory, I think he was the major objector because he was somehow interested in the Safari at the time."

109

Wellington had jumped up and seized a plate of biscuits. He seemed extremely agitated. As he swung round to offer them to me, a good half fell into my lap.

CHAPTER SIXTEEN

"Were you covering the Safari?" I asked Otieno when I had de-biscuited myself and Wellington had subsided. Through the uncurtained window behind him I saw the lights of planes landing and taking off at the airport.

"It was the big event that weekend. Being a Sunday paper which came out on Saturday we couldn't do much more than bring the leaders back to Nairobi at the end of the northern leg on the Friday night. Basically, my job was to feed stuff—interviews, background and so on—to the guy who actually wrote the story. The main thing I remember was the so-called 'duel to the death' between Joginder and Nowicki, and I got some good quotes from Joginder. I think he went out of his way to help me; there weren't that many African sportswriters in those days.

"It wasn't till the question came up in Parliament and it was my turn to write 'Sporting Chance' that it occurred to me to focus on what seemed, looking back, to be the real story: your parents' fate."

"The mystery of car 48."

"Yes. It seemed odd that such a potentially human

interest piece—I'm sorry, but that's the way our minds work in this business—should've had such scant coverage."

I asked him how he'd found out as much as he had. Apparently the Clerk of the Course made the record available to reporters on a routine basis. Information on the bash on the front of the car he'd got from a friend at police headquarters who'd sneaked a look at the official file, which was classified. In order to protect his source he asked around and came up with at least two witnesses who'd been at Ena Bridge and could vouch for it.

Names? I pricked up my ears. But Otieno had long since discarded his notes, and had only hung onto the piece itself because, as he joked, it represented Lesson One in the political education of a sportswriter, a book he hoped to write in the unspecified future. He had a notion that one of the corroborators was a driver he'd met covering a local rally and the other was an official or a bystander. He suggested checking the Clerk of the Course's records for useful names, like the drivers who'd overtaken car 48 on the Chuka to Ena stretch mentioned in his article.

Another fact gleaned from his police friend he hadn't been able to use in the end because corroboration was impossible: a 5-gallon drum full of petrol had been found inside the crashed car. This was unusual for a couple of reasons. Few drivers carried extra fuel because of the weight and the risk. Rather they would plan their refuelling stops in advance, which was exactly what car 48 had done;

in fact friends were waiting at Embu to fill it up. Secondly, the drum contained not regular petrol, but high octane airplane fuel. To use it would have spelt disaster to the Humber's motor.

"What was in the tank?"

"Yes, I wondered too. But it was unadulterated petrol. They had filled up in Nakuru."

What, I asked, were the chances of seeing the police file. Otieno didn't hold out much hope. His friend had left the force to work for a brewery. He didn't know what the reaction would be to an open request, but fancied it might not help my immigration status since basically the same people were running things. The inspector at Embu at the time was a sad character, a *Mzungu* who'd chalked up a grisly record of extracted confessions during the Emergency, when Kenyans—particularly in the Mount Kenya area—were fighting a grim war against their British overlords. "A colonial hold-over," Otieno called him, "who was still fighting Mau Mau in the forests." His theory, clung to obstinately to the Department's embarrassment, was that my father had been abducted by unregenerate Mau Mau forest-fighters. This had led to his finally being forced to quit the police and the country for the more hospitable environment of Ian Smith's Rhodesia.

I asked Otieno if he remembered anything about the hat and pipe that were supposed to have been found at the scene. He did. They had variously placed my father fair and square in the car at the time of the accident, or had been planted there by somebody to mislead the police—depending on the particular theory subscribed to. Another detail he remembered was that no prints at all were found on the bowl of the pipe, which seemed to have been wiped clean. Also, the tracker dog had simply not picked up my father's scent outside of the car. Granted, it had rained, but mostly before the accident.

Had my father himself been a suspect in my mother's death?

Otieno let his eyes fall momentarily. "There was a warrant out for his arrest."

Somewhere nearby a baby had awakened and was whimpering. I heard the pad of footsteps and the hum of soothing words. It was time to go. I stood up and held out my hand. "Thanks very much." I meant it.

"I wish you good luck," he said.

On the drive back Wellington was remarkably silent, as if some weighty matter exercised his mind. I had a fair idea what it might be. To lighten the gloom I asked him about his family; but his replies were evasive, as if I was probing some dark secret, and I gave up.

❧

Hurrying to catch my bus to work next day I was stopped by the morning deskperson. The morning person was more accommodating than the evening person, probably because she didn't have to fend off the swarms of suitors that cluttered the evening hours. "Did your friend find you?" she asked.

"Yvonne? No, I haven't seen her since yesterday."

"No, no. On Saturday, a short while after you left with that *Mhindi*, a man came asking if you had already gone." I looked puzzled. "A *Mzungu*," she added.

"In a red car?" It just slipped out.

"That's the one."

"Oh, yes. Thanks." Momentum had carried me through the door. I turned and went back in. "I'm sorry, what did he look like?" It was her turn to look puzzled. "I mean did he have a beard, or anything?"

"A beard? No."

"Did he look old? I mean old enough, say, to be my father? Was his hair grey?"

She looked at me oddly, as though I was teasing. "Yes, yes, that's the one." I stumbled out to the road.

That night, after supper, Yvonne came to my room. I hadn't seen her since the trip. She smelt of garlic. "Great news," she crowed. "Take a last look round."

Involuntarily, I did, at the mustard walls, the thin orange bedspread and matching plastic chair. "Why?" I was suspicious.

"We're quitting this fleabag. Setting up house on our own."

"Oh yeah. Where?"

She pointed dramatically through the window at the bombax tree. "Over there."

"Yvonne, you know I couldn't *possibly* afford . . . "

"It works out cheaper. We won't have to pay for meals. We can cook whatever we feel like. I'll show you tomorrow."

"But how on earth did you ... ?"

"Someone at work," she said airily. "It's a sublet, but good for a couple of months, maybe more."

"It sounds fantastic. Too good to be true."

It was. And it wasn't. And the timing was just right too. I'd written to Mrs. Munson in Ravine accepting her invitation to stay, suggesting the coming weekend as it was half-term which meant Friday and Monday off. She cabled back: 'Kibbe To Collect You Daimler Friday.' Since the flat wasn't available till Sunday, by stashing my stuff in Yvonne's room till then and having her move it for me, I saved two days' rent at the Y.

The annoying thing was Wellington. Just as some worthwhile leads seemed to have developed, he had dropped off my radar screen. If he was, in fact, bowing out, the least he could have done was told me. I had to admit to feeling a bit lost without him. Finally, on Thursday, I wrote him a note: just that I'd be away at Ravine over the weekend and at the new flat after that, and hoped to see him. I took it up to Club Jacaranda. As usual, no one was around. I left it on the bar under an ashtray.

Kibbe turned out to be the Munson chauffeur, a wizened man in a proper peaked cap with gold braid along the peak and an air of patient perspicacity about him. His arrival in the Daimler after breakfast on Friday sent my stock at the Y rocketing. It could safely be said that my departure was triumphant and perhaps even that those who had ignored me now wished they hadn't.

Kibbe insisted I sit in the back in lonely splendor and had even locked the front door to forestall a struggle. I had a feeling that he had me precisely slotted. Thus we headed north out of town attracting the stares of the curious. Given a flag and a police escort I'd have passed for royalty, and I must admit I did incline my head a few times and flutter my hand.

CHAPTER SEVENTEEN

T he morning was cold. As we reached the rim of the Rift Valley and began nosing our way down its steep escarpment the mist was slowly rising from the hills above Kijabe, and the top of Longonot, an extinct volcano sitting on the valley floor, was swathed in cloud. Gradually the cloud cover broke and the sun came out and by the time we stopped at the one-horse town of Naivasha it was a beautiful day. Kibbe climbed out and opened the door for me. I entered the unpretentious hotel, sat down at the bar and ordered a bitter lemon; all of which made Kibbe very happy. I had done the Right Thing in what was clearly a time-honored Munson watering hole; I would not be as much of a pain as he'd feared. (Though Mrs. M. would surely have had something stronger.) I knew I needed all the Brownie points I could muster, because when we got to Ravine I had it in mind to request a little detour.

After ten minutes Kibbe put his head round the door and I jumped up, ready for the second lap of our three-hour journey. But there was something I'd overlooked. Kibbe was pointing. Ah, the ladies' room. Meekly, I obeyed. Stepping out into the sunlight I found myself looking along the line of parked cars filled with a sort of shy hope; anything approaching red, and my heart skipped a beat.

Nakuru—an hour later across the bottom of the Rift—was pretty much as I'd envisaged it based on memories of shopping expeditions and a couple of years trundling back and forth to school; the small town to which all other small towns are compared. First the rows of villas with their gardens and views down to the soda lake with its famous flamingoes; then the railway station and the African market and the maze of Indian-owned *dukas*; then the banks, a couple of hotels, the official buildings, set at leisurely intervals one from another.

The stop here was the Club, a stately stone edifice bordering the green expanse of a cricket pitch, to which the Settler families from round about repaired, on 'town days,' to eat, drink and exchange gossip. Kibbe, perhaps sensing that my kidneys were not Munson kidneys, merely asked if I wanted *clubbu*. I declined and we sailed on, past the repair shops where I'd hung out waiting till some vehicle or farm machine was ready, between the vast, lush fields stretching away to meet the broad blue sky, to the Ravine turn-off. Gone was the dusty brown track— scene of many a shattered windscreen from stones kicked up by passing cars—submerged, as Mrs. Munson had warned, under a two-lane layer of blacktop. The new road, coupled with the unusually lush green of the surrounding bush, disoriented me; only the distant Tugen Hills, towards which we made, were any reassurance. And, of course, the signposts, announced by me with great gusto as I learned to read: Campi ya Moto, Mogotio, Marigat, Emening, Baringo . . .

Approaching Ravine I leaned forward and asked Kibbe to stop at the church. He may have guessed the reason for he did not demur, though it was getting on for one and I was probably expected for lunch. We skirted the little square around which were ranged the shops and eating and drinking places of the village, and, changing progressively to lower gears, climbed the small hill shaded by tall gum trees. A clutch of whitewashed government buildings—little more than huts really—were grouped around a flagpole flying the shield and crossed spears of Kenya. Beyond, in its own patch of trees but firmly allied with the powers that be, stood the church (or chapel, really, since it had no spire), of grey stone with sloping tin roof.

Kibbe stopped the car at a gate in a crumbling wall of the same grey stone and I jumped out. The whole place had a crumbled air; grass uncut and overgrown, weeds sprouting from between the stones. A board announced that services would be held on the third Sunday of each month, but its flaked and dulled paint suggested that even this schedule had been abandoned. We had never been a church-going family and I doubt that I'd set foot in the place more than three or four times. It held few memories for me. I walked around to the far side where the graveyard was and stopped dead. There

it stood, a gleaming tower among a slum of other
headstones most of which were overrun by Nature's
tentacles. I approached gingerly, hoping it was someone else's. But no: 'In Living Memory of a Grand and
Dear Lady, Helen Hester Duncan,' and the dates. I
felt my cheeks flush hot with embarrassment. At the
base of the white marble headstone was a reflecting
pool of blue-green gravel with a white marble surround and a border of orange marigolds. Scarcely an
encroaching weed.

I left the churchyard and stood on goat-cropped
grass on the brow of the hill. Spread out before me,
in field and forest and sky and brown and green, I
seemed to see the boundaries of a world that someone, with my name, was part of—never thought to
leave. A double-rainbow spanned the view, like a
proscenium arch, set bright against a steel-grey sky
that sagged with rain. Somewhere over there was
the farm.

"*Mvua takuja.*" I started at the soft, sad voice behind me. Kibbe had come up, and he too stared out-
ward. "*Mvua takuja.*" The rain is coming.

The Daimler purred over a soft expanse of lawn
and came to rest by a bottle-brush tree whose pink
tassels hung limply in the torpid air. The Munson
residence fully lived up to its billing, YE MANOR
COURT, spelled out in wrought iron on the imposing
gates of the estate. Two-storied in reddish, creeper-
covered brick with latticed windows, it would have
faultlessly set off any English country garden;
though in England what sacrilege to drive across a

lawn. Was I anticipating or did my nostrils register
the faint stench of cigar? Sure enough, from the
open French windows boomed the Munson voice,
"*Karibu*, my dear, *karibu*." Mrs. Munson strode towards me, arms outstretched in welcome, and delivered herself of a smacking kiss in the vicinity of an
ear. Cigars and whiskey. "I insist on your staying for
ages, do you hear me? You are to liven us up. We're a
bunch of old fogies now, nothing like the old days.
No one left under the half century."

Over lunch I learned that the candidates for enli-
vening were summoned that night for a 'surprise'
dinner party, and that the 'surprise' was me. Mrs.
Munson quickly divined that I'd brought no suitable
dress and gave me the run of her closets. Standards
must be maintained, here if nowhere else. The
guests must not be disappointed. Rummaging
around, I came up with a black chiffon that could
more or less be adapted to fit my less ample figure.
After lunch I began planning my escape—at least
for the afternoon so I could track down Samweli—
and made the mistake of voicing my intention of
visiting the old farm, some five miles away.

"You'll do no such thing," barked the Munson. "It's
about to pour with rain. Besides, it's simply too de-
pressing, what they've done to it. But if you insist,
and I suppose you do, we'll get Roddy to drive you
over tomorrow. You remember Roddy Mollineux,
don't you?"

Roddy Mollineux. A name woven into the fabric of
childhood by dint of the number of mentions it got

at the breakfast table. "Oh yes, of course." Not that I could pin a face on Roddy Mollineux; more of a feeling. A neighboring farmer. Pigs. A funny smell. Kind of a dark house/horse. Paraffin—that was it—for the lamps, because he didn't have a generator. "Poor Roddy," my mother would say, and people would sigh in a peculiar way. To a small girl, Roddy Mollineux was a bit of a puzzle. The last thing I wanted to do was talk to Samweli with Roddy Mollineux or anyone else breathing down my neck. Rash to have thrown myself on the mercies of Mrs. Munson.

The evening proved either an embarrassing success or a rollicking failure, depending on your point of view. By the end everyone was a bit tipsy. They headed out into the night, a quirky caravan weaving between the trees; not just the vehicles, but their occupants. Old George Slake, who had been Old George Slake when I was a little girl, came with his daughter-in-law who ran the farm since her husband had been run over by his own tractor; the Iversons, Jack and Sasha (who was Lithuanian or Estonian, and had a Tragic Past) and, of course, Roddy. The 'surprise' left people flailing for words, perhaps more annoyed at not having been warned than glad to see me.

"I s-s-s'pose I was one of the last people to see old Dick," Roddy Mollineux confided after we'd stepped out onto the lawn for a breath of air. He had a bit of a stammer.

"Oh?" I faced him, intrigued. He was one of those

older men whose boyish looks stay with them. Ruddy complexion, lank, pale hair with eyebrows to match. Only his neck, I'd observed at dinner, betrayed his age, which must have been mid-fifties.

"That last checkpoint. One headlight out on the old Humber. I asked him whether it wouldn't be wise to change it. Naturally he pooh-poohed the suggestion. Just like old Dick."

"So you were in that Safari?" Here was a piece of luck.

"Was. Operative word. Came to grief somewhat. Ran out of time, to be exact, along with half the field."

"That would have been Ena Bridge?"

"Yes." He seemed surprised that I'd know.

"I've been trying to delve a bit into—well, into what really happened. Did my father seem OK?"

"Oh, there you are," a familiar voice boomed from the house. "Cordial time. What will it be?" We turned obediently. "Don't let Roddy chat you up, my dear. He fancies himself these days as quite the eligible bachelor, though you'd never know it from that jacket. I declare I can hear the moths chomping on it." Mrs. Munson shepherded us to the sideboard. "So it's all arranged then, about tomorrow?"

I opened my mouth, "Uh . . . "

"Of course it is, dear. Roddy, you're to drive Stephanie over to have a look at the Duncan place in the morning. There's a dear. See she doesn't get depressed."

Roddy assented with a little half-bow. When she

moved off, he continued where we'd left off: "Quite his usual self, actually. Puffing at the old pipe, and so on. Too bad." He shook his head, thoughtfully. "Too bad."

CHAPTER EIGHTEEN

T rue to his word, Roddy Mollineux rolled up next morning in what looked to me like a super-sleek racing car, announcing himself with a couple of pips on the horn. Roddy and his car, which, he told me, was a Ferrari, had seemed ill-matched the night before, and at breakfast Mrs. Munson offered at least a partial explanation. Roddy, she announced over her boiled egg, had come into a small fortune from an aunt. He'd always been nuts about cars but had never been able to afford anything decent of his own, "the sort one isn't constantly tying together with bits of string, don't you know?"

We tooled along the narrow lanes. The rain of the previous afternoon had settled the dust and the fields and trees looked fresh and vigorous. "Remember the old clubhouse?" Roddy indicated a wooden hut with the pipe he had now acquired. "Years since we got up a hockey game, even seven-a-side. Had to sell out to the locals in the end, who booze it up Saturday nights. Good time to stay off the roads, mark my words." Up a hill, round a bend, right-hand fork, and we were there, rattling over the cattle grid. In place of the old 'Duncan'–daubed in white inside a plough disk—was a bright green wooden hoarding: FARM TRAINING SCHEME. MINISTRY OF LANDS AND SETTLEMENTS. KEEP OUT.

"Bit of a sh-sh-shambles," Roddy warned. "Theory was to have the chappies who moved onto the old settler farms put in a little time here to see how it's done. Not unreasonable. Chap who's scratched the earth outside his hut all his life and raised a few mealies wakes up one fine day with a government loan and five acres of coffee. He needs a bit of direction. Problem here was management. Farmers keen enough. But you can't get the chaps to run these places properly; too busy having their palms greased to do any *kazi*." *Kazi* means work.

We passed the cattle dip and the old dairy. The fields sloped gently to the dam, beyond which I could see the vivid forest-green of the coffee bushes ranged like the phalanx of an army. I looked for the windsock that used to fly over the old landing strip, but it was gone. Roddy pointed out rows of wooden sheds to our right, new to my eyes: the trainees' dorms. We pulled around the end of some barns onto what had been our big lawn, now gravelled over, a large, weedy, empty parking lot.

The house itself—more a series of thatched rondarals that had mushroomed over the years into a comfortable maze of rooms—had been started by my grandmother during World War One. Her husband, a missionary from Canada, had gone off to fight the Germans in Tanganyika within months of arriving in East Africa, leaving her to fend for herself in

what was then 'virgin territory' for whites. I looked
in vain for some sign, however small, to link this
grey institution to the memory of far-off, happy
days. Even the thatch had been replaced with corru-
gated iron. And, perhaps because it was Saturday,
not a soul around.

Roddy was leaning on a fencepost staring out at
the view. He reminded me today of a sandy-colored
gnome, his worn tweed jacket hanging below the
cuffs of his shorts, his legs brown and hairless, his
face more leathery-looking than last night. I turned
my back on the house and leaned on the fence beside him. The fields here stretched down to a
stream, unseen through the flat-topped thorn trees
that hemmed it in. On the far side were mud huts
clustered in twos and threes. It was here my father
had deeded a few acres to each of our long-time
workers, here that Samweli had his *shamba*. Down
there little white blobs were moving about; the
dress of the local men was white shirts and blue
shorts, or sometimes just a brilliant red cloak. They
would come from the surrounding hills, spears in
hand, to dance for us on the lawn at Christmas.
Beyond stretched the Great Rift Valley—goodness
knows how many miles across—with the sun, catching the hills on the far side, giving the impression
through the blue haze of there being a long white
cliff-face. The view, at least, was the same. It calmed
me.

"What do *you* think happened?"

Roddy knew at once what I meant. "To your parents? Don't suppose we'll ever know for sure."

I pressed him: "Just a guess."

He took a long pull at his pipe. "We all have our pet theories. Old Dick wasn't without enemies, you know. Fact is, he had more than most." He paused. "I think that's a fair statement."

"And . . . ?"

"Did you know that he ran a concentration camp for hardcore Mau Mau detainees for a couple of years back in the 'fifties?" He looked at me. "No, I don't suppose you were even born."

"A *concentration* camp? That sounds awful."

"They were called detention centers. Same thing. It was during the Emergency. He was doing his bit. Didn't we all? Dick had some of the worst offenders in his outfit, killers straight out of the forest. And he didn't believe in coddling the beggars. Discipline and hard work. The public school approach. Mind you, some of the guards got a bit carried away; couple of incidents on work details where they flogged a little over-enthusiastically and the chappy died. Once it got out, there was all sorts of flak; a parliamentary commission came out from London, and Dick was forced to resign.

"When *Uhuru* came in '63 there were chaps still in the forests who expected to come out to a hero's welcome because, after all, their side had won. Or so they thought. Old Jomo had other ideas. He went up Mount Kenya and announced that anyone who didn't come out with his hands up by such and such a day would be hunted down and killed. In the end

most of them gave in, and one or two who didn't
were disposed of in a rather bloodthirsty manner.
But mark my words, there are chaps in there to this
day. It wouldn't surprise me one bit if they hadn't
got ahold of old Dick. He must have been high on
their grudge list, and ten years ago feelings were
running pretty high in Kikuyuland. A lot of people
thought Old Jomo had sold out."

I recalled what Otieno had said. "Didn't the inspector on the case have some such notion and it
didn't wash?"

Roddy tapped the fence with his pipe. " 'Course it
didn't. It's a can of worms they can't afford to admit
to, let alone open. Place would go up in smoke.
Which is why," he tapped his point home again,
"they sat on the whole damned episode." He looked
out over the peaceful valley. "Mark my words, young
lady, appearances to the contrary this country's a
tinderbox just waiting for the spark."

"Then why did you stay?" I knew from Mrs. Munson that all the settlers in the area had had the
option of being bought out by the government so
their land could be redistributed, and most had
gone.

"Because my 'golden handshake,' as they called it,
would have just about been enough to pay back the
bank. Where to go, what to do? On zero? No, I'm
glad I stayed. If you ask me," he leaned back against
the post and eyed his car, "Dick's big mistake was
selling up."

I was inclined to agree. "Why did he?"

"Needed the money. Heck, so did we all. We all had our troubles. We were all up to here in hock to the banks." He touched the stem of his pipe to his neck. "Your father was a gambler. This is one throw he should have bet on. Nairobi," he gave a shudder. "God save us from Nairobi."

While listening to Roddy Mollineux I'd watched a small white blob detach itself from a hut beyond the stream, disappear into the trees and emerge again a few minutes later on our side. As it came towards us across the fields it took on the semblance of a man, an old man but a strong one from his gait as he climbed the hill. It was the way he appeared to have seen us and be walking towards us that first gave me the idea; he was less than a stone's throw away before I was sure: Samweli. But how to dispose of Roddy? "Goodness, it's Samweli, our old houseboy," I exclaimed. "I was hoping to see him."

"Looks like he has the same idea," remarked Roddy. Samweli waved both hands in the air. He was grinning from ear to ear.

"Samweli!"

"*Memsab, 'dogo!*"

We exchanged greetings and news. I asked him how he knew I was here.

"*Nakwisha sikia.*" I heard about it.

"The word is out," said Roddy.

Samweli was looking spic and span in a pair of very white tennis shoes, khaki pants and a spotless white shirt. His once massive face had shrunk with age. And something else was different which it took me a while to figure out: he wasn't in his blue apron. I'd almost never seen Samweli out of his apron. I bemoaned the fact that so much had changed on the farm. "Not one thing is left from before."

"Oh, yes. One thing." He led the way along the front of the house, keeping to the grass, I noted, avoiding the gravel drive. All at once he stopped and pointed into the branches of a great pepper tree. I squinted up, and there, wrapped around a high bough, dangled a few feet of rusty chain—all that was left of 'the longest swing in the world.' Samweli, watching my face, bent double with laughter. So I *had* lived here once, after all.

Roddy hadn't followed us to the tree. The moment had come. "Samweli, show me something else. Is the tennis court still there?" We moved away from Roddy around the end of the house. In place of the grass court with its holey net sagging between wooden posts, a mini forest had sprouted.

"*Miti wa kahawa,*" explained Samweli. Coffee seedlings.

We walked towards them. "Samweli," I went on, in my bad Swahili, "when you were still in Nairobi, after my parents left and before the Italians came, did a *Mzungu* pay you a visit in your house?"

"*Mzungu?*" Samweli shook his head. "No, Memsab." But I had sensed a pulling back in that use of 'Memsab.'

"Odd. Mugwe said that a *Mzungu* came and talked with you."

"You have seen Mugwe?" He deflected the question.

We spoke a little of Mugwe before I tried again. "But why would Mugwe say he saw you talking to this *Mzungu*, when you deny it?"

"*Sijui*, Memsab." I don't know. It was hopeless. Roddy found us wandering among the orange and lemon trees, the fruit of which my mother and I used to make into marmalade together. Samweli recalled how I would stand on a chair by the stove stirring lustily in between tastes.

On the drive back Roddy misinterpreted my silence. "You can't go home again, eh? Isn't that what they say?"

"I didn't think of it as home particularly." Perhaps it was my bad Swahili, and Samweli hadn't understood. I should have had Roddy interpret, just to be sure. But no. No use fooling myself. Samweli had understood all right. He had lied. That was all there was to it.

CHAPTER NINETEEN

It poured again all afternoon. That night at supper I tackled Mrs. Munson about the grave.

"My poor dear, so you've *seen* it. What a perfect shock. I suppose that was Roddy's bright idea?"

I exonerated Roddy. "I asked Kibbe to stop on the way."

"It's so terribly *awkward*. Though doubtless very well intended. Mr. Munson refused to be buried anywhere near it. I had to take him to Nakuru. Of course the Graham-Fortescues appealed to the diocesan council to have it moved, to no avail."

"There's something I don't quite . . . I mean, granted it's ugly, but, well . . . Who did it?"

"Oh my dear, I simply don't know, have no idea, really. Best for you—for us all, for that matter—just to try to forget." Mrs. Munson reached out and tinkled the little silver bell by her place as if signalling the end of a round. A servant shuffled in and began clearing away the plates. We were into prunes and custard before I tip-toed back onto treacherous ground by asking if there was a service in the church next day. No, she didn't think so; regular services had been suspended. The place had been virtually closed since the Graham-Fortescues left, oh, four or five years ago. They'd kept it open by sheer willpower. But she was sure that Kibbe could run me into Nakuru if . . .

"No, it's not that. It's just that I'd like to thank whoever . . . whoever looks after the churchyard."

"Well, I suppose they *pay* someone to cut the grass, or perhaps the goats do it nowadays for nothing." She fixed me with a pitying look. "I'm sure it need be no concern of yours, my dear. *Lete kahawa,* Chuma."

I gave up.

After coffee we went into the drawing room for a round or two of gin-rummy and Mrs. Munson declared her intention of going to bed. As soon as she was safely upstairs, I slipped into the kitchen—interrupting a jolly party sitting around washing down leftovers with bottles of beer—and asked where I could find Kibbe. Instead of telling me, someone dashed off to summon the poor man. When he arrived, his usual imperturbable self, I asked him if he knew who was looking after my mother's grave so beautifully, explaining that I wanted to thank them.

This precipitated an animated discussion. Everyone seemed to have an opinion or comment and I gave up trying to keep track. Eventually Kibbe stepped forward and delivered the collective response: "*Hatujui.*" We don't know. But, he added on a hopeful note, it is said that very early each Sunday morning someone is there cleaning the grave.

Some say it is the wandering spirit of your father; others that it is the father of Memsab Duncan, because he is lying nearby.

"How early?" I wanted to know.

"Perhaps even before the sun."

Before going to sleep that night I set my mental alarm for five o'clock. I reckoned it was three miles to Ravine, under an hour's walk. I'd be back in time for breakfast. Why not?

I didn't fully wake up until I was through the wrought-iron gates of Ye Manor Court and swinging along the dirt road between two low hedges. My mental alarm had let me down. I was a half hour or so behind schedule. Ahead of me the sky loomed orange and pink and grey; behind me it was a deep bluish grey. I kept to the middle of the road—it was drier—and the only sounds were the flip-flop of my sneakers, the weird waking calls of birds and the hum of unseen insects. Once I startled a family of guineafowl who thought they had the road to themselves, and once, rounding a bend, came face to face with two gazelles who looked at me for a cool moment before bounding away over the fields. A little later a yellow cur slunk by, keeping as near to the ditch as possible.

After a while I made out Ravine hill with its rangy gum trees silhouetted against the lightening sky. I could have saved some time, I suppose, by a frontal assault, but had a feeling the path passed too near the old Sudanese encampment where we used to go and buy the bright raffia mats the women made. The inevitable barking dogs might scare away the spirits. I stuck to the road, and, avoiding the silent square, climbed the hill by the avenue of rustling gums.

The flagpole was bare; the government shacks shut up and ghostly. They seemed to exude a coldness as I passed which made me glad of the sweater I'd put on. The church stood forlornly in its overgrown patch of grass, the gate closed as before. I pushed it open. The grass was heavy with dew. As I made my way around the stone edifice I wondered, a little foolishly, why I'd come. I didn't believe in spirits. What did I believe in?

Touching the wall for balance, I peered around the end of what was, in fact, the chancel. My mother's gravestone stood out from its shadowy surroundings, its top glimmering pink as it caught first light, its base still sealed in a pool of gloom. In the gloom something was moving. At first I thought it was an animal, a small deer or a dog, but then, unmistakeably, a hand reached out and clawed the moist earth at the foot of the grave. I pulled back and leant against the wall, breathing hard, the wildest imaginings racing through my mind. It was a good two minutes before I looked again.

The man—it was a man—was in the act of standing up, brushing the dirt off his hands. To my fevered brain, he seemed to be rising from the tomb itself. I thought I heard a mumbled word or two, but it could have been the wind in the gum trees. He turned and the light caught his face. "Samweli!"

I think I scared him as much as he had frightened me. "Memsab?" Thinking back, perhaps he did take me for my mother. People say we look alike, though from that one photo I'd seen, I'm inclined to dispute it.

I walked over to where he stood, a forlorn figure in an old brown raincoat. "What are you doing?" I looked down at the grave. In among the marigolds were pink and blue petunias. "Thank you," I said. "It's beautiful." Samweli began to come to life. "So it's you, who've taken such care of her grave."

He smiled, self-consciously.

"Why?" Long silence. "Is it something you were asked to do?"

"Yes."

"That man who visited you in Nairobi?"

"Yes."

"Was it—my father?"

Sadly he shook his head. "It was not a *Mzungu*."

"Who was it?"

"That *Mhindi*." In Swahili, *Yule Mhindi*; denoting 'the one we already know about.'

"What was his name?"

"I do not know his name."

No matter. I knew. "Why did he come to see you?"

"He gave me money; much money."

"To look after this grave?"

Samweli nodded. "It is so."

138

I squatted down by the marble surround, picked up a handful of the bluish gravel and let it trickle through my fingers. "Why do you think he gave you money to take care of this grave?"

Again, silence; except that the cocks were in full cry. From the direction of the Sudanese village came the harsh bray of a donkey.

"I cannot say." Ambiguous.

"Were they—lovers?" In Swahili: did they love each other very much?

I waited, then looked up at Samweli. Tears were running down his cheeks. He sniffed vigorously, and again nodded.

"It is better that I know these things, now that I, too, am a woman." Trite, perhaps, set down in black and white, but I meant it and it had its effect.

Samweli placed a hand on his belly. "There was a child inside her."

So that was it. I put my hands to my face and sobbed. It felt as if a crust had broken and some deep dry well in me had unexpectedly gushed to the surface; I think at last I saw my mother not as a mother who had failed her child but as a fellow woman, with the complexity and vulnerability I too felt and wrestled with. How long I sat there by her grave I'm not sure, but at some point it struck me that I was alone. I stood up. The sun, a diffused mass of light beyond the trees, had claimed its name day.

Samweli was sitting a little way off against the

church. He scrambled to his feet and came towards
me. "Is the bakery still there, Samweli?" I pointed
towards Ravine.

"*Ndiyo*, Memsab." Yes.

"Call me Stephanie, like you used to. I hate all
this Memsab business."

"*Ndiyo*, Steppy." He never got it right.

Sometimes, on Sunday mornings, we would drive
down to Kotut's bakery in Ravine for sticky buns
fresh from the oven. So we set off, down the hill and
through the square to the one shop that was open,
where the baker—round and shrewd, the same as
ever—supervised his minions wielding great wooden
trays set with loaves in and out of the hot dark holes
behind the counter. I asked for half a dozen buns,
and he waived payment which was just as well; I
hadn't brought money. His son, said Samweli as we
walked away, was now someone big in Nairobi.

A mile out of Ravine our paths divided. I watched
the lone figure trudge off down the rutted brown
road and imagined—every week, for ten years—this
journey.

Mrs. Munson had just cracked the top of her
breakfast egg. "Sorry I'm late," I lied. "Went for a
walk to Ravine and back."

"You *walked* to Ravine?" She looked at me, dumb-
founded.

I put my package on the table. "Sticky buns from
Kotut's."

"Well," she poked at them dubiously with her
spoon, "I suppose they're edible."

CHAPTER TWENTY

"*Kaki na scones na sodah! Sodah na kaki na scones!*"

I'm in Nakuru waiting to board an R.V.P. taxi to take me to Nairobi. A boy is circulating among passengers bound for various destinations selling cakes, scones and bottles of fizzy orange drink. Roddy Mollineux brought me thus far in his Ferrari. He had to bring it in anyway for servicing he said when he stopped by for tea Sunday afternoon, and would be glad to give me a lift. Just as well I took him up or I'd never have met Jerry Coconopoulis. And 'Cocky,' as Roddy calls him, had some interesting observations to make, though I didn't fully realize it at the time.

Jerry Coconopoulis ran a service station and auto repair shop on the outskirts of Nakuru. From some chance remark Roddy let slip I realized they'd partnered each other in a number of rallies, including— here I had to probe a good deal—the one I was interested in. While Roddy was off with one of the mechanics fussing over his transmission, or something, I sat in Jerry's office sipping tea and waiting for a ride into town to catch the taxi.

His name notwithstanding, Jerry seemed about as British as anyone could possibly be, and to prove it had the short-wave radio tuned in very loud to cricket; I gather a test match coming in live from New Zealand. It made conversation pretty impossible, not that he seemed to want to talk. He was the strong, silent type. I liked his hands, grease-stained with thick black hair running out along the fingers. All of a sudden he jumped up, lunged at the radio with a fearful curse, and switched it off.

" 'Scuse my French." He flashed one of those instant smiles the British are good at.

Naturally I thought I was to blame. "I'm sorry." I started to get up.

"Sit, sit, sit, sit," he barked, as if I was a dog. I sat. "Rain stopped play. Again. Two hours of play in two effing days." He shook his head grimly.

It was too good an opening to miss. "Talking of rain, I gather you were with Roddy at Ena Bridge the night my parents crashed. Do you remember seeing them there?"

He tapped the desk with a pen. "Ena Bridge. Ena Bridge . . . "

"Roddy said he noticed a headlight was out and had a word with my Dad about it."

"Right. Got you. Ena Bridge. Chaos and darkness. I remember the Humber pulling in. I was trying to raise my wife on the ham radio. We'd gone through four fan belts that night and finally had to quit. Sickening business."

"You're sure it was *them*, in the car?"

He was taken aback. "Yes. I mean, why wouldn't it be? I'd have noticed if it wasn't, I should think."

"Did you see Roddy having a word with Dad?"

"Did I *see* him? No. But I recall his telling me about it. In fact they had a bit of a laugh together. Roddy was fairly chortling over some joke or other, which is sad when you think the headlight could have had something to do with it; not taking the time to change it, I mean."

Earlier, in the car, I'd asked Roddy Mollineux about a remark he'd made about my father being a gambler. "He was a born gambler," he reiterated. "He took risks."

"And Mom?"

"Oh, Helen was expected to go along."

&

The taxi returned me safe, if compacted, to the great metropolis. I must say I was looking forward to the new flat and a talk with Yvonne; and perhaps Wellington had left a message. The change of pace and scene, Nairobi to Ravine, made me feel I'd been away much longer. I was impatient and excited. I felt, for the first time, that I had a hold on something and didn't mean to let it go.

A note on the door said, 'KEY AT Y.' A note with the key said, 'Flew coast back whenever, Yvonne.' Our stuff was stashed in a corner of the living room which also contained a red vinyl couch, two ditto armchairs, a coffee table, some plants, and, in an alcove, a two-plate electric burner, a toaster oven and a tiny fridge. The best thing about the room was the view over the city through a big, plate-glass window. Down a flight of steps to the left of the door were the bathroom and the bedroom, just big enough for two twin beds and a dresser. The place was very new. It still smelled of distemper.

I sat down on the bed by the window. The view here was in the other direction, of the parking lot. It was mid-afternoon on a working day and most of the cars were gone. What to do? I felt depressed. To heck with Yvonne. To heck with Wellington. I couldn't count on anyone. I don't know why Richard came to mind, except that he'd promised to dig up some facts on the sale of the Nairobi home and was one more person who probably had let me down. Still, he'd be in his office now, and I didn't want to call him at home and have to talk to Gillian. It was worth a try, except that the flat was phoneless. (There was a waiting time of over a year for people who didn't know anyone.) En route to the Y I remembered the phone at Club Jacaranda. Aha!

I wandered through the building, opening and shutting doors. Not even the cats showed up. At last, in a stairwell, I found the instrument, inserted my shilling, and dialled the number on the card Richard had given me. One secretary later I was talking to him. "Funny thing, Stephanie, I was actually thinking of dropping by on the off chance on the way home."

"Have you had any luck?"

"Yes, actually. Jolly interesting."

"See you in a bit, then. Oh, how's Gillian?"

"Any day now."

As soon as I hung up it dawned that he didn't know I'd moved. I was out of change, so, pitting hope against experience, I dialled again. The call went through. I left word with the secretary. Another of Wellington's little secrets laid bare: the office phone. Before leaving I checked the bar to make sure my letter had gone. It had.

According to Richard, when he showed up at the flat, the house had been in *my* name. The deed transferring it from my father to me was lodged at the bank. Richard hadn't actually seen it, but a friend at the bank had read it to him over the phone. It was dated February, two months before the accident. "Does that surprise you?" he asked.

I said it did.

"Well, this may even more. The proceeds of the sale—quite a substantial sum—were paid into a joint account in Canada in your own and your guardian's name. Payments were made over four or five years to satisfy regulations here about capital transfer overseas."

"Stone a crow," I said. So all this time ... It figured. We were standing in the parking lot as Richard didn't want to be too long away from a phone, just in case. "Why would they do that, put it in my name?"

"Could be fairly obvious." He sounded uncomfortable.

"Well?"

145

"Apparently your father had, well, had got himself fairly heavily into debt. Having as few assets as possible in his own name would insulate him from the collectors."

"I see." I'd never really known what my father had done in Nairobi those last two years. ("God save us from Nairobi," Roddy Mollineux had said.) "So what happened to the debts after he—disappeared?"

"Apparently they were paid. Anonymously." Richard sounded puzzled. "Better scoot. Can't keep the next generation waiting."

I watched him swing the Porsche out of the lot and up the road. Perhaps I'd misjudged the man.

Yvonne walked in to find me frying sausages. I had been down to the shops and bought a few essentials. She'd already eaten, she said. I had to listen to the whole saga of her coast fling before getting a word in about my own much more mundane weekend. Lamu was fabulous, she said. She'd slept on a flat roof under the stars. The dhows were majestic. The sand was golden. The coconut palms whispered in the ocean breeze. The people moved gracefully when they moved at all. For all I could tell, Yvonne had spent the weekend flicking through the *National Geographic*. I yawned. "Oh yes, Steph, and we flew right over a herd of elephants!"

"Wow," I said, for the fifteenth time. By the way, guess what, Yvonne! Kassim was my mother's lover; she was pregnant when she died; I've had a letter from my Dad; he's here in Kenya; oh yes, and my guardian embezzled my inheritance. Of course I didn't say it in so many words, but it all came out. I even showed her my father's 'letter.'

Yvonne hung, open-mouthed, on every word. "I don't believe it," she kept muttering. Still, her concern seemed quite genuine. And it felt great to have someone to talk to about it all. "What are you going to do now?"

"Get a hold of Wellington," I said, "if I have to put an ad in the paper."

I drifted off to sleep to the yowling of the Siamese. Louder than ever. If I said it once, I'll say it again: that cat is living on borrowed time.

CHAPTER TWENTY-ONE

Heather, as usual, beat me to the office. "Oh, Steph," she glanced furtively at Miss Hickle's door, "a *man* phoned. He left a message."

"For me?"

"He wouldn't give his name."

"What was the message?" *Wellington!* About time.

" 'Roddy—with a Y—Roddy knows.' "

" 'Roddy knows'?" Not Wellington. "What did he sound like?"

"British. Serious. He said you'd understand."

"He did? Well then I guess I do." She looked at me a little enviously. It had crossed my mind more than once that Heather led a tame life: she was dropped off every morning and collected every afternoon by her husband and always brought the same lunch, a tomato sandwich and a Kit Kat. But I wasn't about to explain things to her. I wasn't sure I did understand what was happening. Roddy knows *what*? I thought about it and thought about it and by the end of the day all I could come up with was Roddy's Mau Mau theory—the one the inspector pushed that wouldn't wash about my father being on some grudge list going back to the Emergency.

I was walking down the school drive to catch my bus home when a car slithered up alongside me. Wonder of wonders: a battered blue VW with Wellington Waki Oloo in the driver's seat reaching over to open the curbside door. I got in. In the back seat was a small girl. "You have been lost," exclaimed the private eye for hire.

"*I've* been lost? I'm not the one who's been lost." I must have sounded properly indignant. "Didn't you get my note?"

"Oh yes," he said, sorrowfully. "It is very difficult for me."

"We need to talk. I'm in the new flat now. We could go there."

"We cannot talk in that place." His sureness surprised me.

"Oh? It's just Yvonne and me."

We were heading downtown. "We will go to my house," he announced.

I must have sensed he had disagreeable news because I launched right into the saga of my Ravine weekend as if to forestall whatever it was. I talked. He drove; through the downtown area, out past the railway station, the African market, the football stadium and rows and rows of little brick and concrete houses to which the workforce of the town was traipsing after the day's exertions. Wellington was very quiet. I didn't think he'd heard a word I said.

"Twelve thousand shillings for an educated one." This, in a most dismal tone, was his sole comment. His mind was clearly elsewhere.

We pulled up behind a long line of cars at a stop-
light. He gave me a mournful look. "For this
amount a good second-hand car is possible. Not
third-hand, not fourth-hand. I mean a plaything
that has just gone from Westlands shopping center
to Muthaiga and back. Finish. A Toyota or even a
small Peugeot."

"What are you talking about?"

"I am talking about the going price for a nice
bride in this country. It is going into the roof."

"Why? Are you thinking of getting married?"
(Then whose are all these kids, including the one in
the back seat?)

"Please. I have enough. It is for my son, who will
soon finish with the university. Of course she should
not be very well schooled. Not a PhD. for instance—
that is for big people. For my son, a nurse maybe, or
at least a form four leaver. Perhaps five thousand
shillings would do. And a *ng'ombe* or two." He re-
lapsed into gloomy silence.

"Does this have anything to do with our case?" I
was beginning to sense that it might. We had
turned off the main drag and were zig-zagging
through streets of unenviable squalor and same-
ness, with here and there a social hall or a small
church. Wellington's right arm, hanging out of the
window, seemed to have taken on a twitching life of
its own as he greeted people in the street or standing in the tiny concrete yards. We must be nearing
home. This was his element.

"That's the whole thing," he said flatly. "It is not

our case. It is *your* case. This is what I have to tell
you. Last week I was sacked from it."

I had feared as much. All the same, it was unlikely he had dragged me all the way out to the loca-
tions—as these tracts were called—just to tell me
that and complain about the cost of wives. He pulled
up at the curb and leaned back to open the door for
the girl who shot out and disappeared between two
houses as he yelled last-minute instructions. "I
found things he didn't want me to find."

"Like his suppression of Otieno's story about the
accident? I think we've the same person in mind."

"The selfsame. I too learned from a certain watchman about his friendship with your mother. Many,
many times she came there for a visit. When he
hired me he told me to help you, not dreaming that
Wellington Waki Oloo, Private Eye for Hire, would
uncover so many secrets. I am too good for him. I am
too good for my own good. Where will I now find five
thousand shillings for my son's brideprice?"

I knew that sooner or later he would come round
to the dowry. Saddened, I said nothing.

"It is very strange, is it not," Wellington scratched
his head, "that this man who loved this woman is
afraid of finding things out. Perhaps because he already knows."

Knows the truth? I thought of the letter I had in
my pocket. I was now certain that it was from my
father. Should I or shouldn't I show it to Wellington?
I passed it across. "So," he studied it, "he indeed
lives."

"Apparently."

"And you have proof?"

"I haven't seen him, if that's what you mean. I'm not sure I'd know him if I did."

"You are his flesh and blood. You feel him. That is enough."

I'd certainly felt something. It could have been him. Though several times I'd caught myself wondering if someone wasn't just putting me on.

"What are you going to do?" Wellington demanded.

"Basically just find out what happened."

"Would you like some help?"

"I haven't got five thousand shillings. I haven't got five shillings."

Wellington looked at me. "You are too innocent to be here, in this place, alone." I sensed pity in his voice, and resented it.

"I'm perfectly capable of looking after myself."

He laughed gently. "The first thing to do is go back up that mountain. We have to talk to people. In Africa, nothing goes unseen."

"We?"

"Let's say—Saturday?"

"You mean you'll . . . ?"

"I find this case too interesting. My usual work is very dull. Besides," a mischievous light glinted from his eyes, "I have promised these five thousand shillings to my wife already—for our son's dowry. As long as I am on the case I can truthfully tell her to have patience since I have not yet been paid. This will give me time to think of another way to find all that money."

"Wow," I said, and meant it. "Saturday. I'll ask Yvonne."

"No." He was firm. "I think you will find that one has other plans. Now, let us go in."

Our entrance caused a migration of children into an inner room clutching bowls, cups and plates. I remonstrated with Wellington, who shrugged. His wife came back and we shook hands, and I made a complete fool of myself. She didn't look much older than me, so I said brightly, "I don't believe you've got a son in college." She gave a little giggle and disappeared, leaving Wellington to explain. It was his *other* wife—his country wife—who had the son in college. *Father Knows Best* was on TV; in disgrace, I watched reruns till she returned with a kettle and poured warm water over our hands.

Fish stew appeared, and a steaming basin of *ugali*, a thick cornmeal pudding, to mop it up with. Wellington dispatched a child to buy bread for me; he berated his wife for not having any; she scolded him for not warning her I was coming; when the bread arrived—wrapped and white—I refused to eat it. The wife misunderstood, thinking I wanted butter. I felt more and more like Gillian way over on the other side of town. It's all so absurd. Why can't we just get on with life?

Wellington drove me home, letting me off in the road. He would pick me up on Saturday, at Club Jacaranda. When I told him about 'Roddy knows,' he

warned that it was probably a trick of Kassim to put
me off the scent; to make me swallow Roddy's theory
of the Mau Mau abductors when it was quite possibly Kassim himself who had arranged to have my
father kidnapped. I tried to explain to Wellington
that Kassim couldn't possibly know that I'd seen
Roddy Mollineux let alone what we'd talked about,
but he was unconvinced. He asked who else I'd told.

"Just Yvonne."

He laughed, "And who has she told?"

I said I thought he was overreacting, which he
thought very funny. He again told me I was an innocent. "All right," I challenged. "Tell me, what shall I
do?"

"You really want me to tell you?"

"Go ahead."

"Make pretence you have given up; that you have
found out all you want to and are satisfied. Be very
careful about so-called messages with so-called instructions. Don't, above all, mention Saturday."

I was lying on my bed, reading, when I heard a car
door slam out in the parking lot and footsteps tap-
tapping along the walkway overhead. (The flat was
one up from ground level; the walkway reached from
a ramp in the parking lot.) A key fumbled in the
lock. "Anybody home?" called a voice.

"Down here."

Yvonne clattered down the stairs. "Hiya, how's tricks?"

"Fine."

"Had supper?"

"I met a friend. How about you?"

Yvonne nodded, patting her stomach. "If this goes on, I won't fit into my bikini."

"Going away again this weekend?" Say no, I willed. Prove Wellington wrong.

She smiled, secretively. I could have thrown my book at her. "What about you? Going on with the investigation?"

"Uh-uh," I shook my head. "Guess not. I realize it's hopeless."

She bent down and kissed me hard on the cheek. "Oh Steph, I'm so glad. But why? I thought you were really into it." She stank of curry.

"It was getting me down," I said. "I know enough." It was all I could do to let her touch me.

CHAPTER TWENTY-TWO

Next day, after work, I found myself uncomfortably wedged into one of the swings in the children's playground at the Nairobi Rally Club. It was the culmination of a train of events that makes me wince with the pang of remembered embarrassment.

I guess I was, in some areas, a slow developer; and whereas today I might shrug off or somehow make bearable the apparent duplicity of Yvonne (my friend and confidant) and the betrayal of Kassim (my self-appointed protector), at the time I was far too inexperienced in the ways of my fellow beings to be anything but wiped out by it. Confused and helpless fury might best describe the feeling.

I lay in a near catatonic state, the sheet pulled up over my head, for what seemed like most of that night till even the Siamese packed it in. And all the while Wellington's charge danced at the back of my mind. He was right. I *was* an innocent. I backtracked mentally through all the times we'd been together—the three of us, Kassim, Yvonne and I: the night at Embu when she'd slipped away; her jealous pouting when we'd stopped for breakfast by the waterfall; the canopied bed at his house she'd made a point of poking; that time in the market when he'd looked up at the Masai spear. When had it started? How blind I'd been. But what on earth was in it for Kassim, I wondered, that money couldn't buy.

The more I thought, the more furious I became, until I could hardly bear the idea of living in the same house with Yvonne. It seemed somehow obscene. And how had she got this flat in the first place? Hadn't he admitted, that Sunday he first came over, to an interest in the building? Innocent! My God. Nudged by these feelings, a fantasy—something bold and daring and not at all innocent—took hold in my mind and grew with all the convenience that angry and self-soothing fantasy provides.

I pictured myself brazenly entering the bar at the Rally Club, a sort of holy of holies since it had been out of bounds to me as a child. Remembered glimpses conjured up a secret grown-ups' world, the glint of colored bottles, the click of billiard balls, sudden bursts of laughter, the smell of tobacco and beer I associated with kissing my father goodnight. I visualized seating myself with seasoned self-assurance on one of the zebra skin stools at the bar, unrecognizable behind designer shades, silk headscarf and ruby-reddened lips. "Just waiting for someone," I murmured. In my fantasy I smiled alluringly at the bartender polishing already gleaming glasses; not that he had questioned my right to be there. With a white skin you could get away with murder.

"What's your poison?" A man sits down beside me.

"Gin."

The man signals to the bartender who sets down a bottle. "Cheers." The man downs one glass, then another. Obviously he has seen it all and has tales to tell; a veritable Hans Christian Andersen of the rally crowd. I cozy up to him, and repeat in answer to his question, "Just waiting for someone."

"Anyone I know?"

"Perhaps—Mr. Kassim Salim."

"That bastard! What do you want with him?"

"He invited me to meet him here."

"You don't want to get mixed up with him, young lady. Are you married?"

"No."

"Well, believe me, you'd best stay away from him. I've seen more virgins laid waste by that Don Juan of the rally circuit than there are cylinders in a Daimler. Something about his eyes that women just can't resist."

"But he seems so nice."

"Nice, eh? Ten years ago in this very clubhouse he seduced a wife and mother; such a wonderful woman too. Yes. Lured her from her husband, and when he tired of the affair he killed her. Very cleverly. Made it look like the husband did it. Oh yes, he's rich, has influence; he had the whole thing hushed up."

Fantasy merged into fevered sleep.

Whatever possessed me to stop in at the Rally

Club after work the following day I do not know. But stop in I did. It was something resolved on in a heated moment I simply had to go through with. The place seemed faded, utilitarian, not at all as I fancied it, with little plastic packets of peanuts and stained cardboard coasters. The Happy Hour seemed to be dragging: a couple at darts; three men at a table; myself, awkward and out of place, at the bar. I had just decided to slip ignominiously away while the bartender's back was turned when the dart game broke up. The man stopped to chat with the group at the table; the woman approached the bar. She seemed a mild, middle-aged, unintimidating sort of person, with a dash of vivacity.

"Hello." Conscious, perhaps, of my scrutiny, she addressed me. "I don't believe we've met."

"Hi," I blurted, adding defensively, "I'm just waiting for someone."

"Oh?" she smiled, "anyone I know?"

For a ghastly moment as she looked at me I fancied recognition lit in her eyes. In my bag I actually did have a pair of Yvonne's designer shades and wished devoutly I'd had the nerve to put them on. "I don't suppose so," I heard myself mumbling. "He's called Kassim Salim."

"Good gracious," she exclaimed. "Not old Kassim! Aren't many around here who don't at least know *of* him. I haven't seen him in absolute donkey's years." The bartender set a drink in front of her and carried one around to where the man had now pulled up a chair with the others.

"I thought he was a member," I stammered. There was no retreat.

"He was; he gave it up—oh, years ago. Quite tragic. But perhaps you know the story."

"I've only met him once. I'm with the Peace Corps," I lied glibly. "He promised to show some of us his old car collection." It rolled right off my tongue.

"Lucky you. Not many get to see it. He has some real gems, they say. As good as money can buy. He's kept very much to himself, since the accident."

"What accident?"

"Oh, one of those things, you know. People falling in love; one of them already married; happens all the time. It would have blown over, I'm sure, only she went and got herself killed in a smash-up on the mountain. Her husband was with her and just disappeared. Never been found. Kassim took it very hard, it seems."

"But you don't think Mr. Salim had anything to do with it?"

"The accident? Kassim! Dear me, I didn't mean that." She leaned towards me, lowering her voice. "He was the third leg of the stool."

"And the husband," I pressed my luck. "What about him?"

"Older. Bit of a rough diamond, really. Though I must say he did wonders with the club theatricals. Livened up the panto no end. I'll never forget his Widow Twankie. One can't help wondering what ever in the world happened to him."

Her partner had come up and was pointing at my empty glass. "What'll it be?" He was told the news. "Kassim? I'll be dashed!" Surprise, more than enthusiasm, here. He flicked his fingers for the bartender. "G&T?" He, too, fixed me with that slightly searching look. "Kassim, eh?"

"Thanks, but I'd better see if he's coming. Nice meeting you." I fled.

And that is how I came to be sitting in the Rally Club playground with my backside wedged into a child's swing. More than likely the very swing I'd mooned away the time in—legs already too long for the swing but years too short to be inside with the adults—all those years ago. That's where I was, I suppose, while my parents' marriage was falling apart.

That night I waited up in hopes of seeing who or what delivered Yvonne to the flat. Each time I heard wheels on gravel or the slam of a car door I switched off the light and stood watching at the curtained window. I needed some hard evidence to convince myself once and for all that she was what she appeared to be. Each time, a false alarm. At last I gave up and drifted towards sleep. A strange quiet pervaded the night. It bothered me. Just before dropping off the edge I realized what was wrong: no Siamese. Yvonne hadn't made it home before I left for work in the morning.

Getting back, I saw signs that she'd been and gone again—or that someone had. Her drawer was pulled out; I guess for a change of clothing. As I walked through the parking lot an altercation was at full throttle. A man I hadn't seen around—who turned out to be my neighbor—was accusing the old watchman of doing away with his cat. The watchman sat under the bombax tree and shook his head philosophically, as if he'd been accused of worse crimes in his day and survived. No corpse had been found. I suggested a cooling-off period. Cats have a way of coming back.

That evening the man knocked at my door, I think in search of a sympathetic ear. He was, he said, an Ethiopian who'd had a Ford dealership in Addis Ababa. After the Emperor and the established order were swept away he'd fled south in a late model pick-up with the cat and twelve hundred flintlock muskets which he hoped to sell as antiques to a collector, perhaps in Texas. Did I know anyone? His wife and small son were still in Ethiopia. He was arranging to have them smuggled out. We chatted for an hour and he promised me an Amharic meal. Were the guns stored in his apartment, I wondered.

When I walked in after work on Friday Yvonne was throwing some things into a carrier bag. "Taking off?" I enquired.

"For the weekend."

"The coast?"

"Amboselli. But next weekend it's Lamu again, Steph. It'd really be neat if you could come along."

On the contrary, I thought to myself, it would be extremely messy. Was she serious? No need to disclose my own weekend plans.

࣌

At last, the moment of reckoning. I sat at the 'bar' in Club Jacaranda waiting for Wellington. Sensing, perhaps, the special nature of the occasion, the youth fetched me a Fanta orange drink. A good omen. I sipped the warm fizz, then poured an offering onto the floor. The cats sniffed it and stalked away. Wise cats. They know a thing or two.

Wellington bustled in carrying the new plastic attaché case, the one with my name on it. He beamed, brushed aside the proffered Fanta, led me to the VW and held open the door. I was startled to see three little black heads bobbing up and down in the back seat. "They are dropping off," he assured me, as we pulled away.

Drop off they did, at a nice house in a much more upmarket neighborhood than Wellington's. "My brother's," he explained, as the kids scampered up the tree-shaded driveway. "He is very rich, and owns many tin shacks in Mathare Valley. And even some beggars outside the Hilton."

I was shocked, and said so. Mathare Valley is the worst slum in town, a hodgepodge of lean-tos with no city services at all. "At school he was the most revolutionary; now he is the most grabbing," was Wellington's only comment.

Rather than wend our way round the mountain, as before, we headed straight for Embu, on its southern slopes; even so, it was a three-hour trip in Old Reliable, as I dubbed the VW. The car was no speed queen, but Wellington was a dogged driver just as he seemed to be a dogged detective. I was eager to see what he would turn up. To my surprise, I was the one who had the stunning insight, though without Wellington's digging it would never have happened. It was triggered by something Jerry Coconopoulis threw out in Nakuru.

CHAPTER TWENTY-THREE

We only stopped at the Isaac Walton Inn at Embu because of the ladies' loo: I knew it was user friendly. Kenya offers water closets, WCs as they are called, to suit all tastes. Wellington stayed in the car, until I had the idea of buying him coffee and went out and twisted his arm. Breakfast seemed a long time ago.

While we were sitting on the terrace, with a view of where the mountain should have been, a weird thing happened. A man, a perfect stranger, came up and introduced himself. "Aren't you Miss Duncan? You were pointed out the other week when you stayed here. Rather amazing coincidence after you left. Old Polk-Catherway was down from Meru—resides at the Pig & Whistle, straw hat and chins?" He raised a questioning eyebrow. I recalled Polk-Catherway, who'd been control officer, Meru; who knew my parents; who never forgot a face (unless he wanted to). "Said he'd had a bit of a turn. You'd been in with some chappie in a Super Snipe who'd asked about conditions on the old road heading south; split image of your mama, he said you were. Well imagine, he said, a few minutes later, just as he's

165

nicely settled down for his siesta, in walks a chap
the double of your old man; asks more or less the
same thing. Old P-C said he thought he'd died and
gone to Safari heaven! Hyukh-hyukh-hyukh-
hyukh." He squeezed out a laugh. "Can you beat it?
Hyukh-hyukh." His thinning R.A.F. moustache
danced up and down as he backed away, belatedly
aware that perhaps it wasn't quite so funny as he
now told it to me.

Wellington looked rather grave. I tried to smile.

At the spot where the Humber went off the road,
Wellington, though he peered in the direction indicated, didn't seem as interested in the remains of
the car as in the gradient of the road. I reminded
him that ten years ago it had all been murram. He
wanted to know how much the car weighed. A ton
and a half, Kassim had said.

"Phew," he whistled, "like an elephant."

At Ena Bridge he simply asked if it was there my
parents had last been seen alive. Yes, I said. He
didn't even stop, though he looked around with
great interest, having never in his life traveled beyond Embu. "This is the main thing," he announced,
as we headed round the mountain on the narrow,
twisting trail, "what happened between this place
and Chuka. The questions we have to answer are
the two raised up by Otieno in his column, (1) How
did three cars manage to overtake the Humber on
this stretch without ever seeing it? (2) Why was the
Humber fifteen minutes late reporting at Ena?

"From this we deduce two things: that the Humber could not have been on that road at that time at all; yet it started by that way, so it must have turned off on a side road, though within fifteen minutes of the main road because fifteen points at a point a minute were lost." We nosed our way a few miles down every one of some half-dozen tracks that branched off the Ena to Chuka Road. Luckily it hadn't rained the previous day so Old Reliable's much vaunted ability in mud remained untested. She was a plucky little climber, though.

By the time we pulled into the yard at Chuka Full Primary School it was well into the afternoon and I was ravenous. As before, smoke was rising lazily from the headmaster's cottage. With no eating place in sight, I'd have knocked on his door this time and begged for a cuppa and a slice of bread; I didn't have to. We were hardly out of the car before he was coming towards us. I started to remind him of my previous visit, but he broke in right away: "Humbah Supah Sinipe!"

I could see Wellington was impressed. We accepted the immediately forthcoming invitation to tea, and I—rashly, as it turned out—confessed that we'd not had a meal since breakfast. The tea was brought in by a boy who was then dispatched on another mission, I knew not what. Wellington, who didn't speak the language of that region either, nevertheless glanced surreptitiously at his watch. A minute or two later, hearing a kerfuffle in the yard, I spied through the open window the boy chasing a chicken, one of several that were out there scratching around. We were in for the duration.

Lambertus Murungi—such was the headmaster's name—proved something of a Safari buff. When Wellington asked how he knew about the Super Snipe—of which perhaps there'd been less than a half dozen ever in the whole of East Africa and which was now as extinct as Cro-Magnon—a strange and, to me, poignant tale unfolded.

Lambertus Murungi, a fifteen-year old secondary school student ten years ago, had been in the crowd at the Chuka checkpoint that soggy Friday night to cheer the mud-spattered cars as they churned on through, stopping only the briefest possible moment to get route cards stamped. He'd arrived in time to see the leaders, minutes apart as they battled for first place round the mountain; and stayed on till near midnight. Everyone who made it over the hair-pin course as far as Chuka that night was a hero as far as the crowd was concerned. Excitement reigned. But Lambertus had a long walk home ahead of him, so he said goodbye to his friends and headed out on the Ena–Embu road. After a few hundred yards he turned left—the track Kassim, Yvonne and I had driven up two weeks ago—and trudged on. He had the road to himself and kept to the middle, scared, he admitted, of what might be lurking in the dark ditches and hedgerows. Not that he believed in spirits, but he didn't quite *not* believe in them either. For good measure he sang and whistled as he went.

He'd gone a mile or so when he thought he heard a noise behind him. Looking round he saw headlights flashing way off among the scrub; in no time at all a car was hurtling towards him down the road. He leapt up onto the bank and watched it careen by, a big, black car like a charging buffalo. He knew it was a Safari car because of its marking; painted on the roof was a number: 48. As far as he could make out there were two people inside. He guessed they had taken a wrong turn and were lost. He wasn't very surprised, therefore, when, a mile or so later, he heard the car coming back.

But something was different: the headlights were only shining on one side. This time he was able to get in a better position, and as the car passed, still racing, he saw that the lights on the driver's side were smashed in and that the driver was a woman, a European. He walked on. The tracks of the car showed clearly in the bright night, both going and coming; the driver had held a steady course in the middle of the road so that sometimes the tracks almost overlayed each other. But wait! What was this? Human footprints. Skidmarks. One set of tracks veering wildly. On its way back the car appeared to have swerved and skidded, and one of the passengers—the man—had got out and walked around.

Lambertus stood still and looked. Yes, there in the ditch, a strange, bulky shape. He backed away, imagining some hairy beast about to spring at him from the shadows. Nothing happened. He picked up a small stone and tossed it. Not so much as a grunt.

He approached the form and poked it with the stick he was carrying. It felt soft. He inspected the end of the stick, then smelled it. Blood. Whatever it was the car had hit, the impact had knocked it clear into the ditch. Not a dog. Not a gazelle. The hair felt long, coarse and bristly. Perhaps a pig, a big one at that. It's head was in the bottom of the ditch. He pushed it. Heavy. God, how heavy. A pity, he thought, to let jackals and hyenas have all that fresh meat. Pig—if it was pig—was a delicacy. He had passed some huts not far from the road about a half-mile back which seemed to have smoke still coming from them. He would alert the people there; they could come with torches.

The upshot was—Lambertus learned a week later on his way back to school—that the village had feasted on giant forest hog, *nguruwe mwitu,* for three days. He himself had walked on, following the tracks of the car, until, a half mile short of the 'new' Meru to Embu road, they had disappeared into a field, and emerged again—presumably turning around when they realized their mistake.

"That same car went off the road and crashed a half-hour later, just after Ena Bridge," I told him. "Surely you heard?"

"Oh yes," he agreed. "On my return to school I heard very much about it. And, of course, from the number 48 I knew it was the self-same car, Humbah Supah Sinipe."

"Did you go to the police?" Wellington wanted to know.

A bit defiantly, Lambertus shook his head. He had
not told the police. He and his friends had talked it
over and decided he should not. "The inspector at
that time was a very bad *Mzungu*. We did not know
what he would do. The people did not tell him anything. They had seen what bad things he did at the
time of Mau Mau, after people went to him. They
remembered."

Perhaps estimating from years of experience the
time it takes to turn a chicken running loose in a
yard into chicken stew, Wellington asked our host if
he would go with us and show us the road. He knew,
as I knew, that car 48 would not have taken a wrong
turn. "And moreover," he said importantly, "this lady here is the very daughter of those people in that
car."

Lambertus stood up. If he'd worn a hat he would
have doffed it reverently. "The daughter of car 48?"
he whispered, staring at me, his thin face working.

I smiled, reassuringly I hoped. "It was a long time
ago." We headed for Wellington's old *gari*.

"But every day I am thinking of it since that
time," Lambertus said, wonderingly, looking back at
me from the front seat.

Wellington checked the odometer. A little over
two miles down the road we came to a clutch of huts
and pulled up near them. An old man hobbled towards us. Lambertus jumped out and greeted him respectfully and they talked. "These people up here,
they are very strange," Wellington volunteered as
we watched. "Eating dead things from the road."

171

The old man salaamed us and started to talk, all
the time casting curious little glances in my direction. "This old man says he remembers very well the
forest hog. The sweet taste of it is still in his
mouth." (Wellington nodded at me as if to say, What
did I tell you?) "He says the big hogs come down
from the forest at night. They eat our sweet potatoes
and leave only a hole, but this one paid for what he
took." The man wheezed toothlessly. I think he was
laughing. He hobbled away. "I have told him who
you are," Lambertus explained, "and he is bringing
you a present." Wellington looked at his watch.
When the old man returned he handed me a parcel
which seemed to have been hastily done up in a bit
of sacking and old twine. "He is thanking you."

I opened my present: a thick, smooth, brown horn,
eight or nine inches long. "He is sorry, the other one
was broken in the accident." Suddenly I knew what
it was: a hog's ivory tusk. I thanked him warmly
and he went away.

At 5.4 miles from Chuka turn-off we bumped off
the road onto a grassy field, got out and took our
bearings. This was as far as the Humber had come.
Ten years ago, around midnight, this field, unlikely
as it seemed, had witnessed a . . . a what? A something that would tell us a whole lot about what really happened to my parents that night. Rainclouds
were building up, black and massive, while here and
there the sun, over in the west, poured through crev-
ices in golden shafts like a biblical illustration.

"Wait a minute," I shouted, pointing. "What's

that?" Some hundred yards away a lonely pole stood like a bright needle against the darkening sky. All it needed was a windsock. "Is this a landing strip? For planes?"

"Small planes are seen here from time to time," Lambertus allowed.

"I don't suppose one was here about that time?"

"As a matter of fact, it is true. I myself did not see it, but I was told. Even today, if the Safari is coming this way, small planes come here. It is said they are bringing spare parts and such things."

"Are you thinking of that *debe* of high octane petrol mentioned in the police report according to Otieno?" Wellington asked. "So am I."

That yes, and something else.

CHAPTER TWENTY-FOUR

The image of Jerry Coconopoulis reaching angrily for the radio knob in Nakuru came into my mind: rain stopped play.

A rendezvous with a plane at an out of the way convenient little airstrip, planned weeks ahead as soon as the Safari course was announced, planned and rehearsed to split-second timing. So what went wrong? The one thing they had no control over. It was exploding now in fat drops against the windscreen. Rain. Rain stopped play. A bridge washed away, a last minute course change, and the convenient landing strip, less than a mile off the new Meru-Embu road, became an inconvenient landing strip taking car 48 nearly eleven hectic, muddy miles out of its way; not to mention taking the life of one giant forest hog.

So that was how three cars had got ahead of them. Lambertus Murungi had guided us as far as the bridge on the new road, the bridge that had caused the course change. Sitting there in the VW with the first drops ploshing around us and Jerry's words ringing in my ears, it seemed suddenly obvious what had happened. What was not obvious was *why*.

What was the purpose? Surely they didn't go to all that trouble for a drum of high octane gas the car couldn't use? According to Lambertus, the plane had arrived some time in the afternoon and waited. Whoever was in it stayed in it. Lambertus himself had not seen the plane when he passed the spot around midday, nor on the way back after midnight, but he'd heard from local people that it had flown away in the dark with a light.

A suggested visit to Murungi's old mama, who lived three miles into the bush down a farm track, was gently diverted. I asked for a raincheck, then had to explain the term. Wellington was worried about the rain. Perhaps Old Reliable wasn't as good in mud as he'd boasted. Or perhaps he was expected back home that night. I hoped not. There was still too much to learn up here on the mountain.

"Who definitely saw your parents at the Ena Bridge checkpoint?" Wellington asked. We were doing justice to the chicken stew back at Murungi's.

"Quite a few people."

"To speak to?"

"I imagine somebody spoke to my mother when she got the route card stamped. And Roddy Mollineux said he had a word with my Dad."

"Funny."

"They did have a bit of a laugh, yes."

"I mean funny that your mother was the one who ran to get the card stamped since they were in a big hurry and, as the driver, she was farthest from the control officer's table."

"I didn't think of that."

"But I, Wellington Waki Oloo, Private Eye for Hire, although unpaid at the present time, cannot help thinking of it. Why? Because it is my training." He tapped his head. "Do you know what I think?" The stew had done wonders for his disposition. Lambertus listened, wide-eyed. "There was a reason why your father didn't jump out like a gent with that card. He was hurt in that collision with the pig." A look of triumph spread over his face.

"But Lambertus has told us he saw a *man's* shoe-prints in the mud, and that was *after* the hog was hit." I hated to deflate his ego with company present. Lambertus solemnly nodded.

Wellington pulled off a bit of *ugali,* kneaded it into a ball, hollowed it with his thumb, scooped up some stew and conveyed it to his mouth. He chewed slowly and removed a splinter of bone. Lambertus watched and waited. "And who is it who says there was only one man in that car?" Relief and admiration.

We said our thanks and farewells and hit the trail south. Wellington was not a flamboyant driver, but he and the car had an understanding and took the twists and turns together philosophically. In less than an hour we were back in Ena, rattling over the bridge. "From this place to the place of the crash it is three miles," he observed. "Somewhere along those three miles is a clue in waiting to lead us to solve this case."

This was my third time over this stretch of road. I

was hard put to imagine what we might have missed. There weren't any visible villages; a single
turn-off, a half-mile before the crash site, led up the
mountain. To make matters worse, we were running
out of light; in an hour it would be dark. Still, Wellington had said that, in Africa, nothing goes unseen. So far, he was right.

"We will give this old man a lift." We had come
upon him round a bend, shambling along at the side
of the road in a tattered overcoat. Wellington pulled
up ahead and opened the rear door. The old man
climbed in without a word as if he'd been expecting
us. Immediately we both regretted our hospitality.
The reek of *changaa*, the so-called 'native-brewed'
beer, engulfed the car mingling with the earthy
smell of damp overcoat. "Where to, Bwana?" Wellington asked.

The man pointed ahead. *"Juu kidogo."* Up a little.
We came to the turn-off. *"Juu kidogo."* We turned
off. The road forked. *"Juu kidogo."* He pointed. The
car pushed on up the hill. "How much further?" Wellington demanded. The man leaned forward and
peered intently between us through the wet wind-
shield. *"Uko,"* he pointed. There. We pushed on. After another mile, Wellington said, *"Sema wapi?"* Say
where? *"Juu kidooooogo,"* the man pointed. Wellington stopped the car. *"Ondoka,"* he commanded. Out.
The man's eyes filled with tears; he began to plead
in a sing-song pathetic voice; his breath billowed
around me. I was getting a *changaa* high. "We've
come this far, we might as well go on. It can't be

much further." Wellington shrugged. Luckily we'd stopped on a particularly stony stretch; in mud the wheels might have spun. "What work do you do up here?" I asked, as we jolted on. "*Kazi ya shamba.*" Cultivation. "In this forest?" "I used to work at the sawmill." Further on he pointed it out—or what was left of it. "All finished now. No more work."

Beyond the disused sawmill the road seemed to merge into a streambed. Wellington pulled up. "This is it," he said, firmly. Meekly, the old man climbed out. We watched him stagger on up the slope and vanish among the trees. "*Juu kidogo,*" Wellington muttered. Out of the question to turn around here. He decided to release the handbrake and freewheel backwards as far as the sawmill where the ground levelled off. We hadn't gone ten yards when an ominous grinding noise brought us up sharply. We looked at each other and I got out. Wellington eased the car forward and I spotted the culprit: a big boulder had been wrenched out of the ground. And disappearing under the car, bad news—a trickle of thick, black oil.

Wellington dragged the boulder out of the way while I cleared other possible obstructions. He backed down to the flat, jumped out and—telling me to stay with the car—ran off down a path. I was alone in the dusk of an African evening, getting wetter and wetter. The rain wasn't hard, but it persisted, seeming to release a woody essence from the weed-encrusted mounds of sawdust heaped all around. Not much was left of the buildings—the foundations, some low walls and concrete platforms, just a scar in a landscape. Must have been some time since it flourished. A wonderful sadness enveloped the place. I heard a pair of hornbills screeching raucously to each other above the trees and looked up; one behind the other, they were flapping to beat the band as though, if their wings ever stopped, they might nose-dive onto their heavy beaks.

For all I knew, Wellington had gone to relieve himself under the trees. He came puffing back with an old tin can and—yes—a bit of soap and eased himself under the car. Whatever he had in mind it was too late, not enough light. "*Juu kidogo*," he hissed between his teeth. Words which ever after became a private rallying cry between us, a signal for reminiscent laughter. Without that old man's insistence we would never have pieced together what happened on that three-mile stretch that fatal night ten years ago. For the present, however, we were in no mood to laugh, unless bitterly to signal grim acceptance of our predicament.

Wellington, it transpired, had spotted a well-worn path, and—out of sight behind the sawdust—a little homestead with a haze of smoke curling through the thatch. Its occupant, who'd sold him the soap to plug the oil leak, had taken him for a guest bound for a nearby rest house, of which he was the caretaker. No stranger ever came except to stay at the rest house, which had once housed the sawmill manager and was now used by the occasional forestry officer on tour. Otherwise it was rented out to the public.

"We will stay tonight at this place, and tomorrow we shall mend the car," Wellington announced. OK by me. I'd brought a few things just in case.

It was not OK by the caretaker. This petty bureaucrat, miles from anywhere, insisted we must have a *chiti*—a receipt from the Forestry Department in Nairobi saying we had booked the rest house for that night and paid our ten shillings (about a dollar and-a-half Canadian). How could we possibly have booked, I argued hotly, unless we planned to break down at this particular spot on this particular evening? But no amount of logic, pleading or cajoling could separate this wiry little functionary from his perceived function, which was to collect our *chiti*. The veiled promise of a bribe only stiffened his resolve. At any moment—his glance swept the trees—someone with a booking might arrive. The reservations clerk at the Ritz could not have been more aloof. For as long as he had been caretaker, which was very long indeed, no one had succeeded in staying at the rest house without a *chiti*. Wet, bedraggled, we were about to give up when he mentioned that sometimes he forgot to lock the door; if we were to wander in, without permission of course . . . The rascal; I think he'd had it in mind all along. "These people up here are all crazy," Wellington reiterated, as we continued along the path; it was something to do with the height above sea level.

Another few yards and we stood at the garden gate of the cottage; or where the garden gate had once been. Two rampant rose bushes marked the spot. Shorn long since of support, they had piled up on themselves, twin pillars of sweet-smelling exuberance. The house itself was built to last, of stone and tile. The front door opened into a big, dark living room with a fireplace and three canvas chairs, government issue; of three other rooms, two contained iron bedsteads and one a table. The wood-burning stove in the kitchen was choked with ash; the tang of ash and must hung in the cooped-up air. I flung open windows. Wellington, more practical, found a box with two matches left in it. He tried the tap in the sink and unlocked the kitchen door. I heard voices. Outside three ragged little kids stared open-mouthed, then ran off into the twilight. "First," said Wellington, rubbing his hands in anticipation, "we will make a fire."

Some time later we sat with our feet on the hearth, the red glow of the fire reflecting in our faces. There was no other light. A bit of candle Wellington had found in a cupboard and cut in two, we were saving for bedtime. Most of our needs had been supplied by the kids at a price negotiated by Wellington: firewood, eggs, bread, tea; they had even rented us two tin mugs.

It began there, in front of the fire, in idle speculation: what an ideal hide-out this was. Then, I wondered if my dad could have stayed here after the accident.

"Not if that so-called caretaker had anything to say."

"But suppose it was all part of the plan? Suppose he had his *chiti*?"

"Do you think your mother's death was part of a

plan?" Before I could answer—perhaps not wanting me to—he went on. "Maybe there was more than one plan. Take the petrol, the pipe and the hat. The pipe and the hat, by themselves, made no sense. But with the petrol, that's another story, a story that tells me that something went *not* according to plan, to one plan at least." We stared into the fire. "What would you do with a *debe* of high octane fuel?"

"It would make a great blaze."

"And what would you do with a pipe and a hat?"

"Throw them on the fire?"

Wellington clicked his tongue. "No."

"What would *you* do?"

"Save them from the fire."

I saw what he was getting at. "So that people would think their owner was burned up."

"But there was no fire. There was a misfire." After a silence, he added, "It would be interesting to find out if anyone did stay here on that particular Friday night."

CHAPTER TWENTY-FIVE

Walking out into that tangled abandoned garden early the next morning should have been a refreshing experience. Instead, it made me angry. Harebells, hollyhocks, delphinium, pinks, irises, tea roses, phlox: this ghost of an herbaceous border brought to mind my mother, an avid gardener. A life wasted.

As I strolled and picked, a flower here, a flower there—with the intention of taking them back to the flat, knowing that all too soon they would fade—an idea proposed itself as if whispered in my ear. Supposing she'd driven over that edge deliberately? Was that what my father was trying to tell me? Was that what he was leading up to, letting me find out little by little as much as I could for myself? What an imprecise way to do it, though. She would know she'd be more likely to be maimed than killed. Besides, where was my father at the time? Had she simply stopped and let him out, then accelerated into the abyss? Perhaps so. Perhaps life had become too complicated. Self-punishment? For breaking her marriage vows? Because of me? And so on, and so on. When Wellington called out that he'd made tea,

I found I had a whole armful of dying flowers.

Sunlight soap, as soap, is pretty devastating; as a temporary plug for a leaking oil sump, it's not bad. It got us as far as Embu, where Wellington paid through the nose, I'm sure, for repairs. I felt terrible about all the shillings he was shelling out, but feeling bad was about all I was good for. I certainly couldn't pay him back. I got to thinking about the money my guardian had stolen from me, and why the house had been left to me in the first place. Was that, too, part of the plan?

❧

Monday morning I was late for work and Heather had called in sick. (It was her turn.) Miss Hickle was either in a cold rage or in one of those purse-lipped states that followed—according to Heather—the receipt of letters from her mother in New Zealand as night follows day. I didn't really care which it was. I had been at the Forestry Department first thing and I had found a name. Conveniently, the office turned out to be a stone's throw from the flat, occupying a maze of wooden huts the other side of Kenyatta Avenue.

The rest house log books were all there, going back years and years, under the stewardship of an official who had no objection to my leafing through them. I didn't expect to see Dick Duncan writ large; most of the people who rented the forestry rest houses had European names, so a European alias wouldn't have stood out. But the name for that particular rest house on that particular Friday ten years ago did stand out because it was Asian: Phiroze J. Latif. He had paid five shillings (the price had since doubled) and signed the book in a small, painstaking hand. I had an idea and could hardly wait to test it on Yvonne that night, if she hadn't lingered past the weekend in some expensive game lodge with her sugar daddy, that is. No, I mustn't be spiteful; she was probably a bundle of innocence.

Driving down from Embu the day before, Wellington and I had had the private eye equivalent of a jam session: we improvised on a theme. Pipes, hats, high octane gas, planes, cars, hogs, footprints, the works, were tossed in and mixed up. But no theory held on every count. Impressed as we were with ourselves, we didn't really cook—or whatever the jazz term is; though Wellington did ask me if I'd be his business partner. It would be "more fun," he said. I could have my own office. "And phone?" I enquired. He smiled, slyly. I said I'd think about it. I couldn't refuse point blank after all the man was doing to help.

Monday evening the Siamese was still AWOL. "That cat," the watchman said with the air of one who knows, "has gone very far." *Mbale kabisa,* his precise words. He pointed in the general direction of Ethiopia. Yvonne, on the other hand, returned. Not wanting to hit her over the head with my burning question in a way that might arouse suspicion, I listened, ostensibly spellbound, to her adventures among the animals that mainly—as far as I could tell—came in VW buses striped black and white like zebras. One bus, she recounted, was stalked by a pride of lions. To the relief of a group from Medicine Hat, Alberta, who were in it at the time, all the pride wanted was their picture taken. "At least they didn't charge," one woman was heard to remark, "like these Masai." I pictured a troop of skinny, long-limbed, spear-wielding warriors advancing in formation. Ours not to reason why.

"Say, Yvonne, do you know anyone called Phiroze?"

"Phiroze!" she blurted. "Sure. I mean, no." A blush spread under her tan. "Who is he?" As a liar, Yvonne was in a league with George Washington and Chicken Little.

"Some guy who came by asking for you." It was my turn.

"Did he leave a message?" I could see she was agitated.

My own face, I hoped, was a mask of indifference. "Uh-uh." Inside, I seethed. Phiroze. Undoubtedly one of Kassim's minions: the diminutive one in the cap, more than likely, who'd accosted me in the post office. Whether he was Phiroze or not didn't really matter; the fact that Yvonne had acknowledged the name—surely not a common one—then denied it, was near enough for me. It placed one of Kassim's people within minutes of the scene of my mother's death that very night. This was something Wellington and I hadn't bargained for. It changed everything.

So pleased was I with Yvonne's performance that I offered to make dinner for us both. Thanks, she said, but she'd just remembered she had to go out again. I could guess where, and regretted my little bit of embroidery on the mythical visit of Phiroze; unwise to have had him actually come looking for her. Just how unwise I was soon to find out.

❧

The week was punctuated by surprises. Since Kassim knew no messenger of his had come searching for Yvonne, I assumed that he assumed I had discovered his little liaison and had a reason for saying what I'd said. Sure enough, Yvonne was dispatched back to find out what it was. She proceeded clumsily, as we lay in our beds side by side with the light out.

"This guy that you mentioned, did he say what he wanted?"

"No." If I had a message for Kassim, now was the time to send it.

"You ever seen him before, Steph?"

"He did look kind of familiar, I must say." Pause. "Hang on, I've got it! Remember on our trip with Kassim when we left you at the hotel in Embu and went to look for the car wreck? It was around there."

Mystified silence. "But I thought you said he was Asian."

I hadn't said he was Asian. "He was a friend of

J.N. CATANACH

Kassim's. He was living up there in the forest." That should do it.

A longer mystified silence. "Then what would he want with me?"

Yawn. "Let me know when you find out."

I had, so to speak, thrown down the gauntlet. Whether rightly or rashly remained to be seen.

The next surprise came the following evening. Wellington and I had set up a system where if I called a certain number and left my name, he would show up at a pre-arranged time at Club Jacaranda, or simply phone at that time to the pay phone under the stairs. That the system worked was a surprise in itself, but the coup de grace was Wellington's news. He had just been offered five thousand shillings to drop the case. Five thousand shillings, the price of a form four leaver.

"By whom?" I asked, unnecessarily.

"A small *Mhindi*."

"With a little cloth cap? Kassim's fixer. I think he's called Phiroze J. Latif." I told him about the rest house log book.

"I will meet him again tomorrow. He is bringing the cash."

I was horrified. "You're not going to take it?"

Wellington smiled. "By no means will I touch it. My brother employs a number of thugs who will grab it. My son will receive a percentage for his dowry. No, I will not corrupt myself with that man's money." Disdainfully he dusted off his hands. I almost believed him.

An exceedingly sober Yvonne greeted me at the flat next day. "What's going on?" she challenged, as soon as I walked in.

"What do you mean, what's going on?" Her face was kind of puffy, as if she'd been crying.

"My weekend at the coast," she moaned. "It's off. Oh, I don't suppose you even remembered." She all but stamped her foot.

"Of course I remembered. I was really looking forward to meeting the boyfriend. It's over then, I take it? Oh well, look on the bright side; it had a long run, comparatively." If she'd opened her mouth at that point, it would all have come gushing out. Her career as an unsuspecting (I gave her the benefit of the doubt) double agent was clearly over. "So Mr. Right he ain't? So what?" I wasn't going to make it easy.

"All this time I thought it was *me* he was interested in. He didn't give a shit in hell about me. He was just doing it to . . . " She burst into tears.

"Come on, Yvonne." I put an arm around her and sat her down. She glared at me through red-rimmed eyes as if it were all my fault, which it was. "I've got to go out again, but I'll be right back and we can go downtown and drown our sorrows in pizza and milkshakes. How about it?"

I walked up the hill to Club Jacaranda. Wellington, as planned, was waiting. "I have been fishing," his chest fairly swelled, "and caught a very big fish." He had rejected the five thousand shillings but, in doing so, gleaned an interesting and unsolicited admission: "My master," Phiroze J. Latif (for it was none other) had said, "wishes to state in a spirit of frank and honest exchange that he was indeed fishing on Mount Kenya on the particular weekend in question, and moreover has already said as much to Miss Duncan."

"He did say he was fishing—deep sea fishing. He has a place in Lamu he goes to. It came up because of the Isaac Walton Inn. He said he didn't go in for trout."

"Could it be that he started by deep-sea fishing at the coast, then flew up to the mountain—it's hardly an hour from Lamu in a plane—and continued with trout fishing?"

"And my parents just happened to be passing and gave him a lift, right?"

Wellington thought this a great joke. As it turned out, the joke was on him.

CHAPTER TWENTY-SIX

T he third tangible message from my father came into my hands—as had its predecessors—in an odd way. The messenger drove up to the flat in a snazzy Porsche. Richard, of course. It was Friday. I'd just got back from work and happened to be changing in the bedroom. I saw him asking the old watchman for directions, and, seconds later, heard the brisk heavy tread of a man with a mission.

"Good-oh, Stephanie." He looked flushed and a bit wild. "Sorry about this"—handing me an envelope— "Couple of hectic days at the hospital. Afraid it's been sitting around the in-tray. Nothing vital, I trust."

"Hospital? Then Gillian's . . . "

"Through the worst. Caesarean, in the end. Tough, but . . . "

"Oh my God. And the . . . ?"

"Fine. Yelling blue murder." He was halfway to the car.

"When can I . . . ?" I shouted.

"Couple of days. When she's out of intensive care." The watchman was holding open the door of the Porsche. First time I'd seen him do *that* for anyone.

191

"Can't I ... " Clunk. The door slammed. " ... help?" I finished lamely.

Richard smiled tightly up at me as he swung out of the lot. I was back in the flat, staring sightlessly over the city of Nairobi before I remembered why he'd come.

'A TAXI WILL COLLECT YOU 1700 HOURS SATURDAY,' the note read; same clipped-out words and letters. 'WE ARE GOING TO THE THEATRE. THIS IS IT GIRL. DADDY.'

Saturday. *Tomorrow.* I looked at my watch. If I hurried ...

From Club Jacaranda I dialled the contact number, left my name and settled down to wait. Chances were I'd missed Wellington for the day. Tomorrow, if I followed instructions, I'd be in a taxi headed God knew where before our usual meeting time. The minutes passed. Twilight turned to darkness. Eyes straining, I copied the message and added one of my own: Wellington could reach me at the flat; failing that I'd be at 'the theatre'—his guess was as good as mine.

I returned home to find Yvonne making dinner. A promising development, considering that the night before she'd watered down a milkshake with her tears. The whole saga of her fling with Kassim had trickled out, from the day—following that first Sunday lunch—that the shadowy Phiroze had picked her up after work, to the terrible night Kassim had scolded her for no apparent reason, and called her a hare-brained slut.

"The beast," I sympathized, gripping Yvonne's hand across the table. "How could he?" Her earlier assessment appeared only too correct: he'd used her as a stalking horse for me.

"He's so lonely, Steph," Yvonne wailed. "He needs me. When these queer moods would come on and the servants were all scared as hell, I could get him out of it."

"So you were off to the coast again, this weekend. Was that *his* idea, asking me?"

She shook her head. "It was going to be a surprise. He really doted on you, Steph. I could tell. Like a father. Always wanting to know what you were up to and everything. He was very concerned."

"It didn't seem, well, kind of weird though?"

"Oh no. I saw the photograph. He had it by his bed. She looked so like you. Just that one time. Then it was gone."

"Like a father, huh?" I picked bits off the pizza. Yvonne toyed with an anchovy.

Now I stood beside her as she stirred delicious-smelling shrimp paella. "That plane of Kassim's. Would there have been room for all of us?"

"It's a four-seater."

"You, me, him—and the faithful Phiroze, no doubt."

Yvonne actually smiled. "Phiroze has never flown in his life and swears he never will."

"What sort of place does he have down there?"

"Out of this world."

"Apart from that. How long has he had it?"

"Ages. I think his father built it."

"Masses of servants, I suppose."

"Just Juma, down there. Juma does everything."

"Is it right in Lamu town?"

"Oh no, it's way up the beach. Quite isolated. He says he goes there to think."

"Pretty cut off, eh? Nothing like a phone?"

"Good grief, no."

"How do you get there?"

"The airstrip's on the mainland. You cross over by boat." Someone was tapping on the door. "That'll be Cyril."

"*Cyril?*" I was halfway across the room. Yvonne waved me back.

"He's a real cutey," she whispered.

I looked at the paella. "I see."

"Oh, you can stay. But Steph, one favor." She pointed at the couch and then at me, closed her eyes and cocked her head.

"I'm supposed to sleep there?"

"Be a sport," she pleaded.

"No way. At least, not tonight. Maybe tomorrow, OK? I'll probably be out tomorrow anyway." That's it then, you're going: I addressed myself. Well, well.

Tap, tap, tap. Sure enough, Cyril.

He had a single preoccupation: biogas. Yvonne sat entranced. To all intents and purposes, biogas was her driving dream. "*Please,*" she hissed, when Cyril was in the loo, "can't you see he's desperate for it."

"Tomorrow," I repeated. The only thing Cyril

194

seemed desperate for was shrimp paella. The poor guy was starving.

"Promise?"

"Promise."

❧

"Right you are, the passenger for the Piper Cub." I had entered the low, wooden terminal building at Wilson Airport, a busy little runway for light planes on the edge of town towards the game park. It was here that my close-mouthed taxi driver had dropped me. The official looked me over, then, adjusting his bifocals, peered out the window to where a number of planes stood waiting in the gathering dusk. A little after six. I was expected. In a last-minute fit of nerves I'd kept the taxi waiting a half hour praying that Wellington would show and even considered tracking him to his house, if I could ever find it again. But the decision was mine and mine alone, and I guess I wanted to go.

An airport worker led me onto the tarmac. It seemed like good weather for flying, not much wind, the odd star beginning to show in a flat grey sky, the sun a red blotch above the horizon. I looked hopefully at some of the bigger planes, two engine jobs with sleek lines and gleaming markings; but no, on we went till only one possibility was left, a wisp of a thing sitting alone in its pool of darkness, a dragonfly on a waterlily pad, the only sign of life a pinpoint of red light on each wing tip; one propeller. "Piper Cub?" My guide grunted assent.

We circled around it to the left, skirting the wing for a side approach. A little flap of a door was open and the man showed me where to put my feet to get in. As I swung myself up I was aware of the pilot's dim bulk filling the cockpit inches from my head. The helmet and goggles could have concealed Jomo Kenyatta himself for all I knew. At any rate, he paid no attention to me. My guide reached up and tugged at the safety belt. I buckled up, pulled the door to and watched him walk around to the front and swing the propeller. My God, I didn't think they did that any more. The machine shuddered to life. Pilot and groundman exchanged the thumbs up sign and we began to move.

The passenger seat was directly behind the pilot's. I could have reached out and touched his shoulders as he maneuvered the craft to the end of the runway. Instead I found something on either side of me to hang onto. I'd never flown in such a small, frail-seeming plane, despite all my father's promises, though it did occur to me, as we paused in our dragonfly, that perhaps he was at last making good. What was it Wellington had said? *You are his flesh and blood; you feel him.* For an instant, as we gathered speed, I felt him. I thought I did. Or maybe I just wanted to so much. Is that you, Daddy? I could have yelled blue murder against the roar of the engine and not been heard. I didn't try.

Ahead were the Ngong Hills, giant's knuckles, unmistakable and black against the evening sky. Incredible to think that down below, on one of those tiny, neat plots, I had sat not many weeks ago on poor Gillian's verandah nursing a gin and tonic. Now Gillian was in hospital in intensive care, and I was nearing the end of my quest. Or so I thought.

The hills flattened out below us and with them went the last recognizable landmark. To the left the sky was blood red where the sun had set; I reckoned we were heading roughly northwest. Craning around I could just see the lights of Nairobi. We weren't aiming for the coast, that was for sure. The plane rose and fell on an invisible swell and gradually my muscles surrendered to its movement. As we buzzed along in a mesmerizing cocoon of noise, it became darker and darker. Not till rain lashed the windows did I realize it wasn't just night we were flying into, it was a storm.

CHAPTER TWENTY-SEVEN

Being out in a Piper Cub in a storm is no fun. A masochistically inclined pilot might see it as a challenge, but as far as the passenger is concerned, sitting helpless in the back, it's like being sealed alive in a coffin and tossed into rough seas. It's pretty disheartening when your mind is trying its damndest to get away from your body, and can't.

I sensed in the turmoil that we were sliding away to the left, perhaps drifting, perhaps trying to work our way around the edge of the storm. After a while I gave up second-guessing and gazed fixedly at a point between the shoulder blades of the man in whose hands my fate rested, willing to him whatever tiny measure of strength I possessed. The rush and rattle of rain against the sides of the plane and the weird moaning the wind made in the framework added to the horror. Lightning tore at the darkness around us. I tried to ignore it, but the thought of being struck and falling to earth like a flaming meteor kept intruding. My right arm felt wet. Was the door properly shut? Was I kidding myself or was the cabin getting lighter, the darkness thinning? Shreds of cloud streamed by. And then—from the cockpit—the thumbs up sign. I felt like touching him, patting him, kissing the spot I had watched for so long; because ten minutes in a Piper Cub in a storm is an age, and, whoever he was, I needed this man terribly.

We were suspended over a wasteland of grey; forest, scrub and grass as far as the eye could see. Not a fire or road or hint of human habitation. Were we lost, I wondered. The engine pulled us on purposefully through the night for another ten or fifteen minutes. It seemed to have no qualms. And then its note changed; little by little we were falling, and as we came towards it the earth appeared to compose itself again; straight lines—fields, a road, even, I think, a railroad. Down, down, down we came; to our left the gleam of water. The plane made a low pass over a grassy field, circled and came in again, lower and lower till—bump, bump, bump—we had landed. We joggled over the grass, then swung around to face the way we'd come. For a moment the machine paused, as if trying to make up its mind, then it rested. We were in a field, in Kenya. Beyond that I didn't know.

The pilot extricated himself from the cockpit, left the plane and walked once around it apparently satisfying himself that it was still all there. He was the right height, I reckoned, and build, and the little of his face that was visible was burned brown. My father's face had had a leathery texture to my probing child's fingers; his cheeks held a number of tiny scars which always intrigued me. It occurred to me

that this was an emergency landing, and we were
going on. But no, he opened my door and beckoned.
As I jumped out, and he removed his goggles and
helmet, conjecture was cruelly stripped away. No
way was this man my father.

Turning, he pointed—at some tall trees that
crowned the ridge of the slope we were on. Good
God, I thought, I know those trees, I've been here
before. I spun around: the dam, the coffee planta-
tion, the landing strip—the farm. Out of sight beyond the trees was the house where I was born. Under those same trees, just two weeks ago, I'd stood
with Roddy Mollineux and Samweli. The angle of
approach had thrown me, and things look so different at night. "See those trees. Beyond them you'll
find a car." He grinned. "Good luck." I was on my
own.

Saturday night. Again, the place seemed deserted.
I climbed over the fence. Not quite deserted: a lone
vehicle was parked in the vast lot that had once
been our lawn and across which, in far off days, the
croquet balls had zinged. We'd played a particularly
vicious game, I recalled, invented by my father, in
which the boundaries were limitless and opponents
grumblingly extricated their balls from flower beds,
long grass and—occasionally—trees. The car purred
to life. My father! Was that him now, in the car, a
red car, circling towards me? Hardly. The driver
leant to open the door: a stranger, a Somali perhaps,
uncommunicative. We swung out of the lot, down
the drive past the farm buildings, the old cattle dip,

the new hoarding, and rattled across the grid. We had joined the road and were starting down the hill towards Ravine when I heard a buzzing off to our right. Twisting round, I saw through the rear window the Piper Cub, lit green and red and low to the ground, veering away down the valley.

I looked at the man next to me. If he heard it, he betrayed no sign. The road was slick, as if the storm we'd flown through had passed this way. He drove fast and with practiced sureness. "Where are we going?" Silence.

The old clubhouse lay like a black sow with a score of cars, like suckling piglets, nestling up to it; the new elite at their 'wheels only' watering hole. Saturday—good night to stay off the roads, Roddy had pontificated. Depending on your business. We slowed to take the turn, then sped on. My driver looked at his watch. After all, we had a curtain to make, it wouldn't do to be late.

Inexorably we climbed Ravine hill, dark under its canopy of gums. The headlights reflected off the smooth, straight trunks, giving them an eerily artificial look. Dread and foreboding weighed inside me, propelling me to a grisly certainty. It was my mother I was going to meet, not my father at all. The District Offices were shut tight, the hill abandoned. For a land where little goes unseen the place was ideally chosen. No casual passers-by up here on a Saturday night, not even a goat.

We stopped at the church. The driver jumped out, motioning me to follow, leaving the engine running.

My puzzlement increased when, instead of walking round the building to the grave, he simply opened the front door—one of those nail-studded wooden jobs that churches have—and disappeared inside. On my two previous visits it hadn't crossed my mind that the place would be open. Yet he hadn't had a key. Odd. Was this our theatre? I hung back, sensing something very final about that moonlit door. How tempting to slip into the driver's seat and take off.

The man reappeared, gesturing to me, tapping his watch. He struck me as being scared himself. "Who's in there?" My whispered demand fell on deaf ears. "Is my father here?"

The man shook his head. "No one is here. You must just wait." Again he disappeared, and this time, cautiously, I followed.

The first thing I made out in the pitch blackness was a small dancing beam of light. I waited till I worked out what it was: a beckoning torch. Edging forward, I came up against a wooden barrier which must have been the rear pew. I found the aisle and, touching the pews on either side, groped my way along. Eight or nine rows to the chancel step. At some point, long ago, those pews must have burst with the strains of "Onward Christian Soldiers" and "Abide With Me." Now only aching silence, and the smell of bats.

The torchlight had wavered to the left where I remembered a curtained area gave some privacy to the priest to don his surplice, and do whatever

202

priests do backstage in an Anglican church. This curtain now was held back enabling the light to play over a plain, wooden chair standing up against the wall. An invitation? I took a tentative step forward. The light continued to play, as though beckoning, over the chair. I sat. My reserved seat. I was catching on. Abruptly the man left, letting the drape fall into place behind him. "How long?" But he was gone. I heard footsteps walking away, the creak and click of a door, the noise of a car moving off.

It was cold in that church. I don't know how long I waited. My stomach growled. More than half an hour, I suspect, before I heard a car coming up the hill. It didn't sound like the red car, which was smooth and quiet. It was more the type of car that announces its presence self-importantly. Hadn't I been in one not so long ago? This fresh sound served to galvanize me. I stood up and groped my way out of the curtained enclosure. Wellington had once let me in on a trick of his trade: never to wait for a person in the appointed spot, always in a place commanding a view of that spot. Something to do with holding the advantage. In the dim light of memory I seemed to see choir stalls across the chancel and inched towards them as sightlessly as when I'd first come in.

The car had stopped. On hands and knees on the cold stone floor I froze. Should I go back? The church door opened, tentatively from the sound of it. Then, for the longest time, quiet. I waited, cursing my noisy stomach, for the latch to drop, picturing whoever it was standing there, peering into the blackness. Then came a single, whispered expletive. "Damn."

Click-clack. The door closed. But was the whisperer in or out? Shuffle-shuffle. Aha. He had reached the pews. Shuffle-shuffle, creak. And sat down. Under cover of his shuffling I had found the choir stalls and crawled in among some very dusty hassocks. We waited in our separate silences, the newcomer's punctuated by little signs of impatience: toe-tapping, stifled yawns, shifts of position; myself desperately fighting a sneeze. It seemed to me that he was waiting for someone and that someone was late. I wondered if the performance had started, or whether there'd been a last-minute hitch.

Again, a car was climbing the hill. The red car, returning. That's what it sounded like. The man in the pew heard it too. He got up, shuffling and bumping his way forward, and sat down some ten feet from where I crouched. I heard a distinct 'clunk' as he placed something beside him on the bench; not a good sound at all. Meanwhile the second car had stopped outside. I waited for the door to open. Waited and waited. Then suddenly it did, and the beam of a torch swung in an arc around the church. I cringed. Steps approached up the aisle, light and sure.

The first man, the one who'd said, 'damn,' spoke in a grumbly voice. "At least yours is working; mine's gone *bure* on me. Typical." Of all people, Roddy Mollineux.

"So what's it all about?" asked a brusque voice. Kassim. I might have guessed.

"S-s-steady on, old boy. What's *what* all about? It's your bloody sh-show."

It was a new and startling voice that answered. "I'll tell you." A spotlight, considerably more powerful than Kassim's, seemed to spring from the back of the church. "Be a good chap, Kassim, and douse that light of yours. Now drop it. Thank you."

A voice from the grave.

"Apologies and all that," the voice continued blithely, "but I wasn't sure I'd enjoy the pleasure of your company on the strength of a pukka invite. And it's rather an important occasion for me. You see, my daughter is among us. You've both had the pleasure, I know. A matter of clearing up a couple of points before she goes back to Canada." That teasing, bullying tone—I'd forgotten how I'd shrunk from it. "By the way, I do admire your *gari*, Roddy; Kassim must be very proud. No trouble winning the big one in that, eh? Which brings me to my first question. (Pay attention, Steph.) Who was in the front seat of the Humber, Roddy, when you had your little chat at Ena Bridge?"

"By golly, Dick," Roddy barely squeezed the words out. "Is that really you?"

"Answer the question, there's a good chap."

"Why Kassim, here," Roddy managed.

"But you thought at first it was me, didn't you? Why, I wonder?"

"He was wearing your hat and s-smoking your

pipe," Roddy rallied enough to sound resentful. "At the time, I thought it was a bit of a lark."

"Until Helen was smashed to pieces a mile or two down the road. Then you thought it was murder. Am I right?"

"Well, y-y-yes."

"And you've been living high on the hog on the proceeds ever since." Roddy did not contradict him. "Kassim, old chap, did you murder my wife?"

Silence.

"Very well, let's try it another way. Did you cause my wife to be killed?"

More silence.

"Look here, this is purely for home consumption. It wouldn't do me much good to go to the police now, would it."

At last Kassim spoke, under the circumstances, calmly, "You know perfectly well I did not murder Helen."

"As a matter of fact, I don't. A man with a clean conscience doesn't submit to blackmail. Give it another go, shall we? Did you kill Helen?"

"Don't be absurd."

"Oh dear, I'd hoped we were going to be sensible." I noted the change in tone. "But just in case, I brought something a little more persuasive."

"If you have a gun, by all means use it," Kassim replied. "In a sense I'd welcome it. But I will never let your daughter think that I killed her mother. That would be cowardice. Whatever else I am, I hope I am not a coward. You know very well what happened. You cannot twist the truth."

Too coolly, "I'll give you a count of ten," my father said. He meant it. I knew from his voice that he meant it. He'd reached nine before I lost control.

I think I screamed, "No!" as I launched myself at Kassim. The shot sang out anyway.

CHAPTER TWENTY-EIGHT

T he smell. I kept coming back to the smell. It had something to do with when I was small. Or was I small? No, I was big. And here was my hand to prove it. Ouch. I opened my eyes. I was lying on my right side staring close-up at an expanse of brown from which grew strands of wiry black hair. My first thought—that I was bedded down with some live creature—wasn't completely accurate; the creature was dead, a stuffed leather couch that oozed horsehair from its many cuts and abrasions. I turned to the source of light: dingy yellow, it filtered through windows that were screened but didn't appear to contain glass, which accounted for the nip in the air. My covering was a worn and dusty Persian rug, laced with dog hairs. On a low table alongside sat an unlit paraffin lamp. Paraffin. That was it. Pigs, dogs and paraffin. Roddy's place. Roddy Mollineux.

I don't remember leaving the church. I suppose I fainted. I came to in the back seat of a car, lying in somebody's lap, strong arms holding me, rather a pleasant sensation. It was dark out. Shadowy figures stood around with lamps as they laid me on the couch. Someone fussed with my shoulder. I remember how it stung. Gingerly, with my right hand, I probed: bandages. I moved my left arm. The shoulder certainly hurt, but not much more than if I'd been stung by a hornet. The elbow worked. I guessed I was lucky.

Knock, knock. A screen door pushed open. "*Jambo*, Memsab." Early morning tea, from which, in the White Highlands of Kenya, there is no escape. The old man seemed well-disposed. I was sitting up quite comfortably sipping the hot brown brew, listening to the borer beetles already at work in the beams above my head, when a tousled visage poked around the door. It was followed by a moth-eaten tartan dressing gown containing the rest of Roddy Mollineux. He grinned foolishly, turned round and stuck his head back the way it had come. From the wheedling and yelping on the other side, it seemed he was staving off a lot of dog. At length he got both the screen door and the other door shut.

"S-s-sleep all right?"

"Pretty good, thanks."

"Sh-shoulder painful?"

"A bit."

He cast around, presumably for somewhere to sit, saw nowhere and thrust his hands deep into his dressing gown pockets. The place was more of a walled-in verandah than a room proper. He surveyed the rusty lamp. "Bloody generator on the blink again."

Come on, Roddy, I thought. Get to the point.

"Narrow squeak." He examined a rent in the window mesh. "Feel like an utter cad."

"Where's Kassim?"

"Toddled back to town."

"He's OK, then?"

Roddy grunted assent.

"Where did my father go?"

"God knows. Damn fool took off like the proverbial bat. Jesus Christ." He turned and gazed through the screen window. "His own daughter."

"Was that true," I asked, after a while, "what he said?"

Roddy scratched an unshaven cheek. "I'll tell you all I know. It's time to stop this infernal guessing game." He continued to stare out the window. "I was sitting in the *gari* at Ena Bridge, waiting for Cocky to raise his Mrs. on the ham radio, when in rolls the old Humber, apparently still in the running. Good sh-show, thought I. So while Helen dashes off to get the card stamped, I stroll over to have a word with Dick. Only it's not Dick. It's Dick's pipe and Dick's old fatigue hat, but in between it's this fellow Kassim. Well, of course, I'd seen him around and so on, but I hardly knew the blighter. To be frank, I thought it was all a bit of a leg-pull and good luck to 'em. So I went right along with it, pretending he was Dick. Not till next day, when all hell broke loose, did I realize I was probably the only one who'd twigged, and there might be a little something in it if I played my hand right. The bank was about to take the farm. I'd have been out on the street. I was desperate. No harm in trying. By gum, if the fellow didn't pay up."

210

"Trouble is," he turned glumly back to me, "chap's been sh-shelling out for something it now seems highly likely he didn't do. Puts me in a heck of a spot. I mean if he didn't do it, I'm back in the hole. How in thunder am I going to pay him back?"

Poor Roddy. I could almost hear my mother saying it. I echoed my father's words: "How can you be blackmailed for doing something you didn't do? It's a contradiction in terms."

Roddy turned baleful eyes on me and slowly shook his head. "Defeats me. But from what old Kassim volunteered last night, I'd give him the benefit of the doubt. Do *you* think he did it?"

"No. Not after last night. Did he say why he was in the Humber, or why Dad wasn't?"

"He did. But don't ask me to repeat it. I'd probably get it wrong. I'm going to stay well clear of the whole business from now on, and I'd advise you to follow suit, young lady. It could get nasty."

"Why?" I'd no intention of taking advice from Roddy Mollineux.

"If you hadn't missed the end of the sh-show, you wouldn't ask. When the shot hit you, your father swore at Kassim that he'd be a dead man if he couldn't come up with proof of innocence within the week. He was berserk, quivering with rage. I couldn't see him, but I felt the heat. Then he left. Just like that. You might have been dead, for all he knew. He didn't wait to find out."

For those few seconds I felt the shreds of a genuine

emotion coming from this pathetic man. "Do you think he's, well, changed? Was this the Dick Duncan you used to know?"

Slowly Roddy had begun to pace. He addressed his slippers. "There's no denying he always had a temper. Got him in hot water more than once." He reached the end of the verandah, turned and seemed to make up his mind about something, "I don't see why you sh-shouldn't know; not after last night. Recall that detention camp I mentioned, and the Mau Mau chaps who were beaten to death? Well, it wasn't the guards who did it. They took the rap. It was Dick."

"Are you sure?" I felt faint. It was a terrible accusation. *Could* my father have done that?

"I was there," Roddy said bleakly. "I was his Number Two." The screen door opened, revealing the ancient retainer who'd brought my tea. "What is it, Apollo?" Roddy demanded testily.

"It is that man," the servant announced in sepulchral Swahili. "The one who came in the night."

"For God's sake send the bugger packing or I'll put buckshot up his arse."

"He is already inside."

"In this house?" Roddy's face convulsed with fury. He made for the door. "Excuse me," he poked his head back around it, then vanished into a commotion of dogs.

Almost at once came a tap on the outside door of my screened-in porch. Craning my neck, I beheld an unexpected sight: the seemingly disembodied head of Wellington Waki Oloo. "Your *simba* is very fierce," he twinkled. I tried, and failed, to respond. He held the door wider. "Let's go." He seemed out of breath.

"I can't ... " The words sounded feeble. Why couldn't I?

"Make haste, this place smells very bad," urged Wellington from the door. I flung off the covers, pulled the remnants of my shirt around me—it had been ripped at the shoulder to get at the wound—and followed my abductor across the rough, wet grass to a cluster of broken-down huts. Behind them, waiting patiently, was Old Reliable. "Lie down here," Wellington instructed, opening the rear door. He looked anxiously at my bandaged shoulder. We bumped along a farm track. The stench of dilapidation hung over the place.

"He has rather a fast car," I warned, "but it's all right. The last thing he wants is a scene."

"Even the rich must breathe," said Wellington slyly, "and the fastest tires need air." He'd thought of everything. And how, I wanted to know, had he found me? We were barrelling along on tarmac before an explanation was vouchsafed.

Wellington, unknown to me, was a champion player in Nairobi's *Ajua* League, a game of skill and speed played with pebbles; in fact he was rated number one in Kaloleni, the section where he lived, and the previous day, Saturday, he had won a six-hour match against Lumumba, a rival section. On finally picking up my message, he'd gone to the flat, found no one, and sensed right away the crafty hand of Kassim. Kassim, the old Sudanese watchman told him, had left his house around 5:30, alone, in a blue Volvo station wagon. A further ten shillings elicited the fact that he had gone to Ravine.

It was getting on for seven. Convinced that I had walked into a trap, Wellington pointed Old Reliable north and stepped on the gas. Just beyond Nakuru he passed a blue Volvo speeding south in the direction of Nairobi with a single occupant who could have been Kassim. It was dark. The Volvo was moving fast. Wellington pressed on. He found the farm, wandered around, couldn't raise a soul, "not even a cow." At the clubhouse, which was packed, no clues—though he found someone who thought he had heard a small plane buzzing around.

In the village itself he had better luck. Two men at a bar said that several *Mzungus* had driven up the hill and then driven down again. One of them was Bwana Mollineux whose Ferrari was well-known locally. Who knew what business they had there? Perhaps just looking at the view. You never knew with *Mzungus*. A red car had been parked in the bushes off the Maji Mzuri road. Wellington investigated and found nothing. He got directions to the Mollineux place where his arrival was heralded by the barking of dogs. It was now quite late. As he sat in the VW wondering if he was chasing ghosts, a light wove towards him through the dark: the tottering retainer. From him, Wellington ascertained that someone answering my description was, indeed, present, but the household had retired to bed. He himself slept in the car—he did look more crumpled than usual—and at first light took stock of the situation. He diverted Roddy by posing as a job-seeker at the front door, then seized his chance.

I added my side of the story.

"So, the big bwana, Kassim, was the one in that car with your mother. Perhaps," he added gloomily, "they were all three in the car. Or perhaps your father was never in it."

"No. It was definitely Dad who went through the Meru control." I reminded him about Polk-Catherway, who never forgot a face.

"Between Meru and Ena Bridge they swapped places."

We were through Nakuru and traffic was picking up. Away to the right the waters of Lake Elementita gleamed in the rising sun. "But why?"

"I could guess," Wellington began, "but if Kassim is blameless, he will tell us himself. At least let us give him the chance. If I am not much mistaken, that insect, Phiroze, is even now searching high and low for me. I tell you, he will have to beg on his knees to me, that one." The prospect seemed to cheer him. "Do you know what this means? It means a form six leaver for my son; perhaps even university level." He leaned on the wheel, urging the car forward.

Something told me that Wellington didn't fully appreciate the situation. I had been there in the church. He hadn't. I had heard that voice. He hadn't. The ache in my shoulder was an all too insistent reminder. I began cautiously. "About your son, there could be a problem. Who is going to sign the check?"

He glanced over and saw that I was serious. "That look you have, what is it?"

I consulted my watch. "Just that my father has a night's start on us. Kassim could be dead by now."

❧

Wellington dropped me at the hospital. I had no faith in Roddy's makeshift bandage, and was feeling a lot more pain. "By the way, you made my brother very happy," he remarked before pulling away. "Those guns agreed with him."

Guns? I drew a blank.

"Those old guns," he insisted.

The twelve hundred flintlock muskets! I had mentioned them to Wellington on our way back from Embu. "What about them?" The brother, it appeared, had bought them from my Ethiopian neighbor, sold them to a group who were planning a coup in Uganda; betrayed the group to the Special Forces, alerted them that they had been betrayed causing them to flee, and resold the guns to a German dealer who was unable to get an export license. All this time—according to Wellington—the guns did not leave the Ethiopian's bedroom. So by the time the original check bounced the poor man was back where he started and Wellington's brother was thousands of shillings richer. A sizable donation to the

Gathundu Self-Help Hospital, Kenyatta's pet chari-
ty, had not gone unnoticed.

"In this way," Wellington said, "we are building
the new Kenya."

"Take care," I called after him. "And look after
Kassim." He waved a jaunty acknowledgment. I
stood watching till Old Reliable was swallowed up
by a roundabout. Kassim. Yes, Kassim. I realized
then what had happened. In that split second, in the
church, I had made a choice.

The saga of the muskets gave me an idea. I convinced the doctor that it was an antique firearm
unexpectedly going off at a friend's house that had
caused the wound. Later, trudging back to the flat, I
caught myself looking about, as if I might indeed be
a target. The events of the night before still bewil-
dered me. What was my father up to? Was it for this
he'd brought me from Sudbury, Ontario, after all
these years? What did he want of me? Was he
crazed? Obsessed? I couldn't figure it out. The one
thing I was sure of was that he was dangerous.

CHAPTER TWENTY-NINE

Yvonne was not welcoming, until she saw my ripped shirt and the bandage. The hospital had done an impressive job and I was to report back every day for a dressing change. "Oh, you poor dearie. What happened?"

"A guy in a church was shooting. I was in the way. It's only a graze."

Yvonne's gullibility knew no bounds. "No?" she breathed. "At communion?"

"Evensong."

"Hey-ho; my little water hyacinth!" a voice called from the bedroom. Cyril. No wonder Yvonne looked flushed and was whispering.

"Has he moved in, or what?"

"Well, only for the time being . . ." She gave me one of her pleading looks.

"Fine, for one third of the rent."

"Steph, he doesn't . . . Oh, before I forget, Kassim was here earlier looking for you."

"For me?"

"Right."

Doubtless it was Wellington he was looking for. "How did he seem?"

"OK, I guess. In a bit of a hurry. Why? What's up?"
"Nothing. I hope. You just go back to your gas man." Sounds of exaggerated breathing from below. I couldn't resist, "Quick. The gas man cometh."

৵

Wellington materialized as dusk was settling over the city. As he predicted, Kassim's men had been out in force since first light, searching for him. He was now on his way to meet with the big bwana—as he called Kassim. Would I come too? I got in beside him. For once there were no kids in the back.

The Sudanese watchman pushed open the gates, one after the other, as he'd done before. As the VW slipped through I fancied something passed from Wellington's dangling right hand to the hand of the old man and disappeared into the folds of his robe. I saw no signs of stepped-up security.

We were ushered by a servant into the airy room where, weeks before, Kassim had insisted on playing the march from the B flat minor Sonata. This evening I noticed one difference: on the white and gold piano sat a lone photo, a face in a silver frame. I went up to it. 'Hi, Mom,' I felt like saying. She wore that deprecating smile where you never knew if she was poking fun at you, herself or a bit of both—disconcerting to a child demanding unmixed emotion. Not so to a woman of twenty-one. I loved her for it. Wellington, too, gazed at the photo.

"You saved the life of the man who failed to save your mother's. My shame is now double." Kassim had come in quietly and stood behind us.

I turned, fighting the impulse to fling my arms around him. "For heaven's sake," I pleaded, "don't let's get mawkish."

The inner courtyard, floodlit, looked like an enchanted garden. Kassim guided Wellington and myself to a sofa facing it; he himself took a seat across from us. He was pale and spoke as though with infinite weariness. "The original equation seemed simple enough, but we were young and foolish," he began. "Helen and I wanted each other. Dick was willing. All he wanted was to get out from under his debts and begin a new life somewhere else. Helen was several months pregnant with our baby. She insisted it have a proper home from the start, free of stigma. For her, this meant marriage. A bigamous one, but this was a risk she was prepared to take. The baby would be seen to be Dick's; I would adopt it. Dick was in a hurry. For him, it was to be all or nothing. The supreme gamble. Not enough simply to disappear: he had to 'die.' He was in a strong position to dictate terms, and knew it. The scheme we settled on was entirely of his design.

"It was imaginative, dramatic even, but basically it was sound. There was one flaw, however, which indeed proved fatal: the weather. As you know, at the last minute the heavy rains forced a route change. I took off from Lamu in good time to find the landing strip that was to be our rendezvous, before dark. Unlike your father, Stephanie, I am not a night flyer. I waited there for hours. It was close to midnight before I saw headlights approaching from an unexpected direction. We changed places without a word. To be honest, I hadn't fully expected him to go through with it. To me it was incomprehensible that any man, however much he profited, could walk away from a woman like your mother.

"In a few words as she drove on she told me about the route change. I was checking the time on my watch when we hit something with an almighty thwack. I remember seeing an animal suspended in mid air above the hood. It landed in the ditch. How your mother kept control of the car the way she did still amazes me. I jumped out to assess the damage: both lights out on the driver's side, a big dent, but the thing was still ticking over. I'd always said the Humber was built like a tank. We raced on. You know what happened at Ena Bridge.

"Once over the bridge I thought we were home and dry. Oh, a fellow at the checkpoint had passed the time of day; but he seemed satisfied I was Dick, and I hadn't the faintest notion who *he* was. I didn't even mention it to Helen. She was wound up tight as a violin, and no wonder. I sensed she didn't want to talk, so we didn't. As planned, she let me off at a turn-off a couple of miles down the road and ploughed on into the night alone. That was the last I saw of her." He looked at Wellington. "How you ever found out I'd spent the night at that forestry cottage stumps me. I underestimated your abilities. Will you allow me, very humbly, to put my fate in your hands? As far as I'm concerned, Dick Duncan—

wild as he may be—has never been less than a man of his word; which means we have six days at the most."

"What did you think would happen, after you got out of that car?" Wellington asked.

"It was simple enough. They'd gone over it a dozen times, Helen and Dick. There was a point in the road where—because of the gradient—a little push could plunge a car sitting on the shoulder over into the ravine. And that was what Helen was going to do. Except that she never reached that point. Before the push she was to have removed three items—the drum of petrol I'd flown up with, Dick's hat and Dick's pipe. Then she'd scramble down, douse the car and set it on fire, mess herself up and crawl back to the road or simply wait for someone to come and rescue her. And that would be the end of Dick Duncan. Helen would go to friends in England for six months, have the baby, come back and marry me. Dick was to fly my plane back to Lamu, spend a night at my house in the care of my servant, Juma, and be smuggled north in a waiting Arab dhow at an exorbitant price."

"And you've no idea what actually happened?"

"As far as Dick was concerned, it was smooth sailing, though I've no notion where he landed up. From that day to this I haven't heard. It wasn't till the following evening that I learned about Helen. Immediately I suspected the car: that collision had done more damage than we'd thought. I had the newspaper I then owned have a photographer take all the pictures he could and from them I tried to piece together what had happened. It boiled down— as far as one could tell—to failure of the steering or the front power disk brakes; or a combination of both. But will Dick believe that? I shouldn't think so for a moment."

Wellington wanted to see the photos.

"Suppose I could rustle them up; they weren't frightfully persuasive. Chap couldn't get close enough. And who's to tell what damage was done at what time? No," he stood up, "we need witnesses. People who saw me get out of the Humber, or saw the car go over the edge. The inspector on the case put everybody's back up with some cock-and-bull Mau Mau conspiracy theory. So the locals clammed up, didn't volunteer a thing, which only convinced him he was right." He clapped his hands and a steward entered with refreshments.

"But weren't you afraid," I asked, "after what happened, that he would suddenly show up again?"

"The accusing finger? You forget, I think, that *he* is the chief suspect. A warrant was issued for his arrest. As far as I know it has not been withdrawn. Besides, why should he? He got what he bargained for; the only one who did."

"Not quite," Wellington put in. "He didn't 'die.' "

"I see what you mean," Kassim looked at him shrewdly. "No, he didn't die. The grand exit eluded him. And there has to be an exit—if I recall my Shakespeare—before the star can return for a bow."

"What was he running away from?" I asked.

223

"He was a complicated man, your father." Kassim smiled to himself. "I suppose one should use the present tense. Helen used to say that his instability was caused by a land mine that went off on an anti-Mau Mau tracker patrol in the Aberdares. It wasn't long after the wedding; they were picking bits of metal out of him for days. To answer your question, I don't know. Himself, I suppose. To be frank, I hardly knew him. We met at rallies, and so on; then, when Helen and I took up—if I may use the term—after they moved to Nairobi, he and I naturally avoided each other. Helen never wanted to leave the farm. She was born there. Her mother, your grandmother, had turned the first sod with a little help from some bullocks. But the government was offering a handsome price and Dick insisted they'd never have the chance again. He was sick of being a poor farmer, he said. So he came to town to make his fortune.

"At that time casinos were the glitter in certain speculative eyes. To put it in a nutshell, Dick backed the wrong group—the Kenyattas favored the rivals—and lost his shirt. He was hopelessly in debt. He had two assets; his house, which he'd had the foresight to register in your name, Stephanie, thus sidestepping his creditors; and, to put it crudely, his wife. We struck a deal. I would see that all his debts were paid, concealing my involvement, and arrange for his 'death'; and she was mine."

A low whistle escaped Wellington's lips. He shook his head. "A very high price, I can say."

"One I paid to the last penny." Kassim seemed to lock eyes with the photo on the piano. "Perhaps to the last drop of blood."

"He's dangerous," I said, "You're right. He's capable of anything."

Kassim shrugged, "Let him come."

As we drove away from Kassim's house Wellington began slowly shaking his head and murmuring to himself. "So shrewd and powerful in business, and so vulnerable and weak in love."

"Kassim?"

"Of course, Kassim. Your White Raj, it seems, implanted in all shades of us a bit of inferiority complex down somewhere inside. It will take a while to exorcize it."

"I don't follow."

"You're still innocent. Stephanie, your father really is a master. What a persuader! He made them think they could get everything they wanted without pain while he went off to new adventures. Or misadventures. Now he is tired of it, of not being anybody. If only he could put guilt on Kassim, he thinks maybe he *could* come out and take his bow. So he aims to persuade you—his flesh—that he really is a great guy who has been put upon. Do you think that by shooting Kassim he will accomplish that?"

"Certainly not," I said.

"So there you are."

"What *will* he do?"

"I think for now he will keep very quiet."

❧

Monday I called in sick and went to the hospital. I waited for an hour to get my dressing changed, then looked for Gillian. She was still in intensive care, I was told in guarded tones by a nurse. "And the baby?" The baby was strengthening by the hour. From the way she said it, I knew that Gillian wasn't. As I was leaving, a figure pushed through the glass doors towards me. Richard. A haggard, unkempt version of the man I'd known. I stopped to say something, but he zombied on by without seeing me.

I had a slight problem of my own: to keep my father from murdering Kassim. So offhand did Wellington appear to be about saving his client's neck that I began to suspect he'd be just as happy to let him die; except for the precious dowry money for his son. He wouldn't want to lose that. "The least we can do is get up there at once and comb the area for witnesses," I remonstrated after we left Kassim's.

"All in good time," Wellington said. "Will they run away, or what? Besides," he surveyed my bandaged shoulder, "this time your coming is not necessary."

That hurt. "Well thanks. I was under the obvious illusion that I was a help."

"Some of these people," he explained not altogether convincingly, "if they see a *Mzungu* they run very far."

CHAPTER THIRTY

Tuesday I went to work. I told Miss Hickle I'd been bitten by a friend's pet monkey. She was unsympathetic. To Heather, I whispered, "Actually, it was a *man*." Her eyes almost popped out onto the keyboard.

Somehow I had to convince my father that Kassim was blameless of my mother's death. Could he be convinced at all, or was I taking it all too literally? I am often accused of being literal-minded. Possibly Kassim's guilt or innocence was immaterial. In my father's eyes, he was guilty before that—of stealing her away, or, worse perhaps—of buying her; a rich man, not even English. Perhaps that was the sin, the punishable offense.

What was my father's state of mind now, today? For ten years, conceivably, he had been planning to stage this vindication of himself in his daughter's eyes. That plan had literally misfired, because few things are as literal as a flying bullet. Where was he now? What was on his mind? What new scheme? It dawned on me that Wellington, in one sense, was right—it wasn't for me to go chasing hypothetical witnesses around Mount Kenya, witnesses that, in my heart of hearts, I knew did not exist. I must find *him*; reason with *him*; show him that I understood; defuse him. That was it, defuse him, like a bomb.

" . . . and that, under no circumstances, can the school be held responsible. Yours sincerely, E. Hickle, Headmistress." The voice droned around my ears like a disturbed bee. "Have you got that, Stephanie? *Stephanie!*"

"Yes, Miss Hickle."

"It must be posted this afternoon, at the very latest." She withdrew to her sanctum. The door closed. I looked at my pad—and saw meaningless squiggles. Heather giggled. I stared at her. She tiptoed over and handed me a piece of paper. "Here. Can you read my writing?"

"Phew, thanks Heather. I was dreaming."

"Lovesick?" she whispered.

I nodded. "It's no good. Besides, my shoulder hurts. I'm going to have to take the rest of the week off."

❧

Wednesday morning I went to Wilson Airport. The night before, in desperation, I'd laid my problem before Yvonne—and, by definition, Cyril, since they were all but glued—in the hopes that an airing would let in some light. We stood at the window looking out over the great, grey city.

"Let's say *my* Dad was out there and I wanted to attract his attention, what would I reckon to do?"

Yvonne mused. "How about a banner? 'Come home, Dad, all is forgiven.' "

"A balloon," Cyril countered, "floating over the building." He started figuring how many hundred-weight of chopped up water hyacinth, when decayed, would generate enough biogas to float a balloon big enough for the word HELP painted on it to be read at a distance of half a mile, and dashed down to the bedroom for his calculator. Yvonne followed, to help him find it. They did not reappear.

Wilson Airport on a warm November morning, cumulus clouds banking up on the horizon, the feel of summer on its way. Wilson Airport, because it was the one place I could think of that he must have left his mark, whatever that mark might be. I was a passenger in a Piper Cub, I explained. On Saturday. I had left my purse in the plane. I was directed next door to the office of the rental company. Yes, the Piper Cub had returned. No purse had been reported. The plane had been flown down to the coast by a company pilot; due back tomorrow. The same pilot? Yes. The same renter? They checked. No. Saturday's client had been a Mr. Gordon Smythe, yes? 'No,' I felt like saying. 'His name's not Gordon Smythe, it's Dick Duncan. He's my father and I'm trying to track him down to tell him it's OK, I'm not blaming him for anything anymore. I want to stop him being hung for murder.' "Yes," I said meekly, "I guess so." And that seemed to be that.

I stood by the side of the road waiting for the bus,

feeling low and dumb and alone. As alone as when I'd stepped off the plane a couple of months ago. Cars and trucks buzzed to and fro. One caught my eye and I tried to focus. It was just another speeding blur, but it was red. It could have been him. Why not? Somehow I wouldn't have been surprised. He'd had me in his sights from the start. For all I knew, that man on the airport bus when I arrived was he. I didn't need to go searching. I was bait. All I needed was a trap.

That afternoon I made a phone call. "Do me a favor, Heather. If anyone asks about me, tell them I'm leaving—going back to Canada."

"You mean the *man*," she whispered, "the one who *monkeyed* with you?"

"Just don't tell the Hick."

At the hospital I had my dressing changed. The wound was healing nicely, I was told. From now on I could attend to it myself. I tried to see Gillian. She was still out of bounds in intensive care; from the nurse's demeanor, perhaps a wee bit better. On the way home I stopped at a travel agency in a hotel near the post office and had them book me on a flight out next day: destination, Toronto. By the time Yvonne and Cyril two-stepped their way into the flat, I was packed and ready.

"Steph!" Yvonne exclaimed, "what's the meaning of this?"

"Isn't it obvious?"

"It's not on account of me, I hope," Cyril remarked smugly.

"Actually, between ourselves, it's a man trap. I

want a certain person to *think* I'm leaving tomorrow for Toronto."

"But you're not?" Cyril sounded disappointed.

"So tonight, Cyril sweetheart, you are taking us out on the town: a farewell blast. You owe it to me, baby, for all those nights on this couch."

"Great idea," Yvonne chimed in. "Where are you taking us, Cyril? I say the Red Bull. I'm dying to go there."

Cyril started saying something about a Wimpy Bar.

"Wimpy yourself!" Yvonne turned to me. "I swear this guy is the cheapest son of a yellow cur I ever set eyes on this side of Yeppoon." I had a feeling it wouldn't be long now before I got my bed back.

We shared rack of lamb at the Red Bull—Yvonne and I, that is, Cyril had the tofu salad—and followed it up with dancing at Parrot's Beak. Yvonne and I danced together while Cyril sulked at a table with his calculator and a glass of water, apparently weak from spending money Yvonne admitted she didn't realize he had. "I can't think what I saw in him," she yelled as we thumped and gyrated, shoulder notwithstanding, to the latest beat from Kinshasa. "On the rebound, I guess."

"From Kassim?"

She nodded, a little guiltily.

"Is he really a great lover?"

"Kassim? Full marks, in some departments."

I studied her face for clues, but the music seemed all that mattered.

I am still on the couch. Cyril, condemned, is spending his last night downstairs, though I doubt he knows it. It is three o'clock in the morning and I am suddenly wide awake, wondering why. I hear nothing unusual. Insects, the odd car. Oh God, the cat! The cat is back and yowling right outside the door. I hadn't seen the Ethiopian recently. Was he away? The Siamese used to jump in and out of a little window he left open high in the wall. Perhaps it was closed. I was on my feet wondering what to do, when I heard another sound; further off, this one, from the parking lot—human. Someone was hollering.

I emerged in time to see a man making for the road. Struggling into my bathrobe, I dashed down the walkway and through the parking lot. As I reached the road I heard a car starting up and headlights flared in the dark. I ran out as they came towards me down the hill, holding my arms wide in a futile gesture of command. He had to slow down or risk knocking me over, but he didn't stop. "I don't blame you for anything, Dad," I shouted. "Don't you understand!" But he was past me, the red car gathering speed. I stood there, on the verge of tears. Then, in the distance, loud and clear, came that special salute—toot-toot, toot-toot-toot, tooot tooot tooot! I'd heard it last ten years ago standing with Mugwe, our cook, by the roadside in front of the house, watching the Humber's receding tail lights.

"*Mvua takuja,*" Mugwe had said, as he hurried me indoors. The rain is coming. It was the last I saw of my father.

Yvonne found me and led me back to the flat. Several people had ventured out to see what the matter was. Two or three hovered around the watchman who sat under the bombax tree looking grey and shaken, but with the glint of victory in his eye. He too had been awakened by the cat, I later learned, in time to challenge the intruder.

In the morning—after ejecting Cyril and before she left for work—Yvonne remembered something. "Did you drop this? Somebody picked it up in the hubbub last night." A creased and dirty envelope with my name scrawled on it.

As soon as she'd gone, I ripped it open. 'Stephie girl,' I read, 'the audience didn't ought to take the stage, you know. And, by the way, I wasn't aiming to kill the bastard. He'll have to wait till Saturday for that. I'm not your old Dad, you see, not any more. I'm someone else, somewhere else, you wouldn't want to know. Not a nice person at all. Think of me as then—not now—if you have to think of me at all. But at least you now know the truth. Over and out.'

Thank God I was alone, because these words had a weird effect. I screamed. I swore as foully as I knew how. I looked around for something to smash, screwed the letter into a ball and dashed it against a plant. Then I wept. I suppose I was a little girl again, throwing a tantrum over things I couldn't bear and couldn't change.

Came a tapping on the door. I didn't answer. More taps. "Yes?" I managed. It was the Ethiopian, concerned. "It's OK," I assured him through the door, "I scalded myself."

"You were right," he said, "the cat came back."

After a while I retrieved the screwed up letter from the floor, smoothed it out and re-read it: a hurriedly hand-written note. I have it still.

CHAPTER THIRTY-ONE

"Till Saturday," the letter said. It was now Thursday. Under the circumstances I did the only thing I could think of: I waited for Wellington. He had promised to contact me at the flat one way or another as soon as possible. As everyone discovers sooner or later, if you wait for something long enough it never comes, so I immersed myself in solitaire. I was down seven hundred and some points when I noticed that a shoe had planted itself on the floor at the edge of my vision; a man-sized brown leather shoe, dusty, with a brownish trouser cuff comfortably draped about it.

I didn't look up. "Wellington?" At first, silence; then the throaty gurgle of delight I had come to know. "Never, ever, do that again. Please."

He sat down in the middle of the couch. "We private eyes have a saying: a locked door is an open invitation."

"I happen to know it wasn't locked."

"That's exactly the thing; but how would *I* know if I didn't try it?" He beamed. "Are you not happy to see me?"

"Should I be?"

"I have come to request the pleasure of your company at a little reception for . . . "

"Excuse me," I interrupted, "but aren't you forgetting something?"

"Oh that," he said dismissively. "It is all fixed."

We were talking at cross purposes. "I mean the witnesses. What happened, for heaven's sake?"

"I told you: no problem." He sounded as though witnesses were ordered by the yard.

"You mean you found someone who actually saw the car go over?"

"Not one, many. If not, how could I afford such a big party to launch my son on his marriage prospects to a university leaver, which I am trying to invite you to?"

"Wellington." I was not in the mood for games. If the man was out to be cool, he came across as coy. *"The witnesses."*

"It is well known by certain people up on that mountain what happened to your mother. Because of circumstance, however, these people were afraid and kept quiet. Had they spoken, they feared very much being arrested and imprisoned for the murder of a white memsab. The Humber, you see, broke before reaching the proper place. Your mother, worried in case of the last minute failure of the plan, paid some men very much money to push it to the edge while she steered. Perhaps these men had drunk too much *changaa*, perhaps she paid them too many shillings, who is to say? They pushed that car too quickly, and pushed it over the edge."

It tallied, as far as I could tell, with all we'd come to know. And yet . . . Perhaps that was the problem. "Will he really believe that?"

"Your father? My assistant is even now tracking him down. When he is found, we will go to him, myself and you, perhaps tonight, perhaps tomorrow."

"Not me." I shook my head. Puzzlement, but also compassion, spread on Wellington's face. "Besides, you'll never find him."

He smiled, somewhat smugly, I thought, as if knowing something I didn't. "Speak for yourself."

"I tried, not very successfully."

"I know. You were clever the way you pulled him out. But the jackal follows the stalking leopard in order to taste some fresh meat. While intent on you, he is himself being observed."

I stared at him in amazement. "So you didn't go to Embu at all?"

"Who says so? You are jumping, Stephanie."

"Even Wellington Waki Oloo, Private Eye for Hire, cannot be in two places at once."

"You'd be surprised. In my home district I have seen it. A *Mzungu* who managed a sugar estate became convinced that when he turned his back his *watu* relaxed too much. So one day he took out his eye and put it on a post and went away. The men kept on working. So you see, I learned something from you people."

"Except that you don't have a glass eye."

"Better still, I have an assistant."

I capitulated. Whatever Wellington was up to, he was steps ahead of me.

"And I have three people who are willing to swear before your father that they pushed that car too far."

"But that's incredible." I glanced at the door. "*Here?*"

"Nearby," Wellington allowed. "It is costing me too much already. These country people who come to town think they can have a VIP expense account. They eat nothing but roasted goat, insist on Rhino Beer, and take only Somali women."

I assured him that Kassim would reimburse him generously.

"So you will not come to see him?"

"It wouldn't help." I handed him my father's note. "We've said goodbye."

He read it, wordlessly.

"How is Kassim? Have you seen him?"

"He is strange, that one. He sits at home, hoping that your father will come."

"I knew it," I said bitterly.

"I have my people posted," Wellington smiled. "The goose at all costs must be saved," he patted his pocket, "until the egg comes out."

As the day drew on, so did my sense of helplessness and awful doom. I was alone in the flat. Nairobi through the window—sunny and inviting—seemed unaware of the fragile ties that might be mended or shattered in its streets that day or in the days to come.

The knock at the door came in the middle of a long afternoon. I wasn't exactly expecting Richard, but neither was I surprised to see him. He had played messenger before. He looked a lot more put together than the day he'd passed me at the hospital; yet I knew at once his news was somber, and with an engulfing swiftness I blamed Wellington. If only he'd listened . . .

"Musn't stay," Richard said, "there are a thousand things to do. But I wanted to tell you myself."

"Not . . . ?" I choked, tears flooding my eyes.

"Gillian died last night. In hospital."

I threw my arms around him, sobbing freely, not letting him squirm free; sobbing partly—I am ashamed to admit—with relief, so sure had I been it was Kassim, and that my father had been arrested for his murder.

Late in the afternoon I ventured out to the store beyond the post office. The Ethiopian was coming to dinner, an attempt at atonement on my part for all the false hopes I'd raised in the affair of the muskets. And to take my mind off other things. Trudging back through the parking lot in the gathering dusk I was startled to see Kassim, deep in conversation with the old watchman.

"Where have you been?" He greeted me almost gruffly, explaining that he'd been to the flat and found no one.

"Shopping."

"At a time like this! And here I am, worried half to death that you'd been kidnapped. With good reason, it appears. Our friend here has described your father's nocturnal visit. If I hadn't insisted that unknown people—of whatever hue—be challenged, one dreads to think what might have happened."

"You're the one he's after," I protested. "You shouldn't be out like this."

"But don't you see? That's what he *wants* us to think. This man is devious. No Stephanie, I've thought it over. It's you he's after. If he can't convince you he was right, your very existence becomes a constant reproach. Myself, I am of little consequence."

We had walked away from the watchman and stood by the foot of the ramp leading to the second floor. "Come home with me for a day or two till all this blows over. You will be well protected."

Tempting. At least that way I could be sure *he* was safe. But something still bothered me, something I had to have out with him first. "Why should I trust you?" I blurted. "You used Yvonne, didn't you? For just as long as it suited, then you let her go."

To my surprise, he laughed. "Yvonne is nobody's shrinking violet. You could equally say that she used me. Still, I take your point. In my concern for your safety I was forgetting the unbridgeable chasm that lies between us." He turned to go. "But promise me, Stephanie: no more shopping. Not till our friend Wellington sounds the all-clear."

"Only if you promise too."

His hand went to his heart. "I do."

Moments later I heard the sound of a car starting up. I did not look back, nor brush the tears from my eyes. 'Blown it again, Steph.' Dinner was a culinary bomb. The Ethiopian, ever the gallant, seemed to savor every mouthful. Yvonne, if she hadn't been so busy captivating him, would have been more honest.

CHAPTER THIRTY-TWO

I was as good as my word. Friday and Saturday passed like lost days. On Sunday afternoon I set off up the hill to Club Jacaranda where I was to meet someone who would take me to Wellington's party. Not that the festive mood was on me. No word had come from Wellington since Thursday, and the news of Gillian's passing tinged everything with sadness. Sweet, precocious Gillian, who had seemed to lack nothing.

The thud of a drum sounded nearer and nearer and round the corner towards me trooped the little chanting band I'd come to expect each Sunday at this time. Dressed all in white, white banner held aloft daubed red with a cross and the name of a sect, their ecstatic faces always managed to disturb me. Perhaps it was the certainty they expressed. And today—for it is late Sunday night as I pen this final entry in my diary in the bedroom overlooking the parking lot—today more than ever I feared them. Suppose I stood my ground and held them up, like a policeman stopping traffic: *would* they stop, or, unseeing, dance across me?

> *... for the world, which seems*
> *To lie before us like a land of dreams,*
> *So various, so beautiful, so new,*
> *Hath really neither joy, nor love, nor light,*
> *Nor certitude, nor peace, nor help for pain ...*

The bumpy, unpaved strip leading to Club Jacaranda was lined with cars, among them Old Reliable.
I pushed open the door and heard music and the
gabble of voices, and closed it again thinking I'd
wait outside. But a head emerged and a hand beckoned: a spruced-up version of the youth with the
dustrag. He ushered me down the corridor and held
open the door. An out-of-order sign hung on the
phone, I noticed. The big room was transformed, ta-
bles and chairs dispersed in little groups between
potted palms, well-dressed people standing and sitting in animated discussion, spilling out onto the
patio; a small band playing as one or two couples
moved lazily on a rug-sized dance floor; the bar well-
stocked with beer and soda. Somewhere, something
good was cooking.

"*Karibu, karibu,*" a familiar figure bustled towards me through the crowd, slapping hands, flashing smiles. "Surprise, isn't it?" We shook hands and
he swept the room with proud gaze. "Just as I told
you, all these people here have come to catch my
son. They are people with disposable daughters.
Come, you must meet him yourself personally." He
took my arm. I did not want to meet his son, I want-

ed to find out about my father and Kassim.

Halfway across the room a man backed out of a group and blocked our way. Wellington—reluctantly, I sensed—introduced us. "My grabbing brother," he declared amidst much hand-slapping and joshing.

"Who is grabbing?" The man, sleek and jolly in a shimmering sharkskin suit, held onto my hand. "So this is the one," he wheezed with laughter. "No wonder you are keeping her all to yourself." He turned to me. "It was a nice tip; oh yes, a very nice one." I could hardly see his eyes so deepset were they in fat.

"He means those old muskets," Wellington murmured, dragging on my other arm. But his brother's grip was firm.

"I trust that any small service I may have been able to render in return was satisfactory." I think he winked.

"I'm not sure I follow."

"Come, come, don't say my brother has grabbed all the credit." He let go my hand. "But I trust he will now relinquish a portion for me."

"Credit for what?" I asked Wellington as he pulled me away.

"It's not important."

I stopped short. "Then tell me." We had reached the patio. He sighed uncomfortably. "Those witnesses: there were none. I just borrowed them from among his thugs."

So that was it. "My God," I choked. He might as well have punched me in the stomach; yet hadn't I known, all along, that something was wrong.

"Perhaps she *was* pushed in that way. Only your mother could tell."

"But my Dad: he'd have smelled a rat a mile off. If you tell me you saw him and he fell for it, I won't believe you."

"I saw him. In fact I saw him on Thursday after we spoke. Whether he smelled or did not smell, he accepted it. He is a proud man looking for a way out. I offered him the way."

"*Thursday*? Why didn't you tell me?"

"It seemed a pity. Was something nice not trying to happen?"

I must have blushed, because Wellington beamed. "Where on earth did you find him?"

"The Norfolk. We might have guessed."

"And he wasn't any trouble?"

"I intimated that the authorities had their eye on him, and that they might strike at any time; just a friendly tip in his ear."

"And do they?"

Wellington seemed surprised at the question. "I've no idea. As for him, he didn't wait to find out before taking a night flight to Khartoum. Perhaps the curtain had come down and he heard no clapping, only boos."

"And Kassim, is he . . . ?"

He read my mind. "Let's say he was very well this morning, when he signed the check."

"He didn't . . . ?"

But Wellington's attention had wandered. "Ah,

here is my son. Dalmas," he called out, "I would like to present Miss Stephanie Duncan."

An earnest young man, immaculate in suit and tie, peered at me through strong lenses. "So you're looking for a bride," I remarked absent-mindedly as we shook hands. My thoughts were elsewhere.

"Yes indeed," he responded with enthusiasm. "A simple country girl. That's the thing for me."

Behind him I saw Wellington's face fall. Gradually, as word spread, the lively buzz of talk that had filled Club Jacaranda dwindled and died. People started remembering other important engagements they had to rush to. From the road came the noise of drivers revving their engines.

From where I write I see the bowl of the night watchman's pipe every so often glow orange as he draws on it. Is it imagination, I wonder, or do I smell the night blossoms now covering the bombax under which he sits?

A few days before Christmas (I was contemplating the return to Ontario in this, for me, bleakest of seasons) a friend from my Y days—a Zambian on a typing course—brought over a letter which, she said, had been pinned to the notice board in the hall "for some days."

'Miss Stephanie,' it was addressed, 'The Daughter of Car 48, c/o Y.W.C.A., Nairobi. Dear Miss, Much greetings to you hoping that you are pushing on well. If at some future point you are passing by this way, please look in. News of a pressing nature awaits. I thank to God of this opportunity to write this missive to you. Yours faithfully, Lambertus Murungi, Headmaster, Chuka Full Primary School.'

Early in the new year I drove with a friend from the baking pavements of the capital into the comparative cool of the eastern slopes of Mount Kenya, and once again found the headmaster at his post. I admit I'd had misgivings about the urgency of the mission, recalling his yen for company, but the summons proved amply justified.

Some weeks after my visit with Wellington, word having spread, Murungi received a visit from a stranger. This man, now retired, had been an *askari* or guard at the District Commissioner's *boma* at Embu. One day, a few weeks before the running of the Safari, he was discreetly approached by a certain *Mzungu* he had noticed on a number of occasions at the *boma* and promised much money if he would wait at a certain spot on a certain day and perform a certain deed. One third to be paid in advance and the balance later. On the appointed day, at the appointed spot, the *askari* hid in the bushes near the edge of the road with a sharp panga. He waited till after midnight but the thing which he was told would happen did not come to pass. At length, tired and confused, he gave up and walked home. When, next day, the news of my mother's accident spread, the *askari* was very much afraid that blame would fall on him. For ten years he had kept his guilty secret. Now he had come forward to cleanse his conscience.

Murungi opened his fist and let drop onto the table a dirty, pink, hundred shilling note. "He is returning the payment."

I could only stare in horror at the crumpled ball stained as it seemed to be with my mother's blood.

Naturally I was keen to meet the man and hear the story with my own ears, but Murungi apologized: the man did not wish to talk to me. And that was that. Sitting there in that quiet compound among the trees, my thoughts in turmoil, I felt for the first time that my place was here in Kenya, and that leaving would be running away.

Ten years have passed since the events in this narrative took place and I am still here in the land of my birth and my mother's birth, whose sod my grandmother as a young bride had broken with a plow. And what of others?

Yvonne married Roddy Mollineux. She fell in love with his Ferrari at Gillian's funeral and by the time she met Roddy it was too late; she resigned herself to the fact that he went with it. A baby was born to her on their farm, a boy. Each time I visit the lad looks a little blacker, but if she knows who the father is she isn't saying. Yvonne has done wonders with the farm and Roddy potters around and is ignored, even by the dogs. When Samweli had to give up tending the grave, Yvonne took over. The ivy she planted is a great improvement.

Richard wanted to marry me, but I managed to deflect him as gently as possible. He needed a mother for his daughter more than a wife. He stayed on in Kenya for a year or two before being posted away. We still write. He was a great help gathering the necessary papers in the suit I brought—and won—against my guardian. Some months ago he was posted to one of the Gulf Emirates and wrote of a meeting with a man—"a pathetic case, a bit of an Ancient Mariner"—who had grilled him for an hour about Kenya and "seemed to know everyone." In his last letter he mentioned this man's demise, which was truly grotesque. Apparently he'd wandered, crazed, into the desert where his flyblown corpse was found, half eaten by dogs. Strangely—ominously, some will say—I felt nothing. He was no longer my father; he wasn't even the man who tried to kill my mother.

Club Jacaranda was bulldozed away and an aggressive tourist hotel has risen on the site. As for Wellington, he continues his enigmatic self, appearing before me out of thin air like the genie of the lamp. Often he will set out a particularly knotty case, hoping to obtain what he calls "the perspective of innocence." In truth, I think he finds me a refuge from the claims of his growing family.

For myself, keep me away from the B flat Sonata and I'm OK. Visitors sometimes ask what the bit of yellowed tusk is that floats around this house. I usually think of something. This morning, for instance, a man came about some kittens I'd advertised (yes, I inherited the Siamese) and I was using it as a doorstop. "A reminder," I replied, "that 'the best laid schemes o' mice and men gang oft agley.'" Only Wellington really knows. With typical tact, he calls it, "The Instrument."

I married Kassim. It took a couple of years for it to happen; a couple of years for two stubborn souls to face the fact that each was loved by the other "till death us do part." But that's another story.

The text is set in Century Schoolbook, which evolved from a type cut in 1894 by Linn Boyd Benton (1845-1932) in collaboration with the American printer Theodore Low De Vinne for his Century Magazine. Accommodating the basic tendencies of the modern face, Century improved upon its readability by thickening the true modern's hairlines in the so-called Egyptian style. While retaining the large x-height, Century Schoolbook is a modified design resulting in a less condensed, highly readable face. It is one of only three new text faces cut before 1910 which remain in use today.